THE DREAM OF A BEAST

D1147224

THE DREAM OF A BEAST

$\int \int$

Neil Jordan

CHATTO & WINDUS
THE HOGARTH PRESS
LONDON

Published in 1983 by
Chatto & Windus · The Hogarth Press
40 William IV St, London WC2N 4DF

British Library Cataloguing in Publication Data

Jordan, Neil
The dream of a beast
I. Title
823'.914[F]   PR6060.06255

ISBN 0-7011-2740-6
ISBN 0-7011-2741-4 Pbk

Typeset by Inforum Ltd, Portsmouth
Printed in Great Britain by
Richard Clay, The Chaucer Press,
Bungay, Suffolk

Kill not the Moth nor Butterfly
For the Last Judgement draweth nigh.

WILLIAM BLAKE

1

When I came to notice it, it must have been going on for some time. I remember many things about that realisation. Small hints in the organisation of the earth and air, the city. Everyone was noticing things, remarking on things around them, but for me it was critical. Change and decay seemed to be the condition. It wasn't always like that, people would say while waiting for the white bus or circumventing the mounds of refuse that littered the pavements, but from the tone of their voices it seemed just a topic of conversation; the way once they talked about the weather, now they talked about how 'things' got worse. It was during a summer that it all quickened. There was the heat, first, that came in the beginning and then stayed. Then fools who for as long as I had known them had been complaining about wet Junes and Julys began to wonder when it would end. The pavements began to crack in places. Streets I had walked on all my life began to grow strange blooms in the crevices. The stalks would ease their way along the shop-fronts and thick, oily, unrecognisable leaves would cover the plate-glass windows. And of course the timber on the railway-lines swelled, causing the metal to buckle so that the trains were later than ever. The uncollected bins festered but after a time grew strange plants too, hiding

1

the refuse in rare, random shrubberies. So they had plenty to complain about, no doubt about that. For my part though, I didn't mind too much. I had always liked the heat. I took to wearing a vest only, under my suit, and walking to work along the buckled tracks. Those trains that did arrive I took advantage of, but for the most part I took advantage of the walk.

But then I've always been a little simpler than those around me. By that I mean that people somehow, even friends of mine – perhaps mostly friends of mine – would find plenty of chances to laugh at me. I had never minded their laughing. I accepted it. Things they seemed to take for granted I found difficult, and vice versa. Tax-forms, for instance, I could never fill out properly, so I would put them off until the writs began to arrive. Neither has gardening ever been my strong point. But give me a set of elevations, give me a thumbnail sketch, give me a hint of a subject even and I can work wonders with it. I often wondered: had my eyes been given a different focus to most others, so that while we looked at the same scene all right we saw quite different things? And of course people laughed, they will laugh, even get indignant, as when the tea you make is weak or you burn the toast only on the one side.

So when other people noticed the heat, what I noticed were the soldiers. I often wondered if they thought they could control the heat by having more of them around. Or were people succumbing to the leaden days in ways that were alarming? They were getting younger too, with that half-shaved look that kids have in their teens. Mostly on their own, never in groups of more than two or three, you'd see them keeping guard by the tiphead shrubberies, or walking the opposite way to everyone walking home from work, as if obeying some other plan. Is there a reason for it all, I wondered, that they don't know but that those who have plotted their movements know? And my memory of the time of my first realisation is connected with one of them.

2

There must have been a white bus that day. I didn't walk along the tracks anyway because I was walking up the roadway from the concrete path by the sea. I was walking up past all the gardens to my left and there was the sound of all the sprinklers hissing when I saw one of them inside the gate. He was as young as the rest, and dark-cheeked, bending over a rose tree. His khaki shirt was damp all over the back and under the arms. I could see his nostrils almost touching the petals. He is as alert as an animal, I remember thinking, or something inside me thought. There was the smell of just-cut grass. All the gardens stretched away from him, like wrapped boxes waiting to surrender the scents of their rose-trees. Then a door in a house opened and the soldier straightened himself, but not fully, for he slouched out of the garden and down the road. Underneath the rose-tree, I could see now, there was a pile of cut grass and a dog curled in it. I saw his long cheek and his glistening nostrils. They were flaring with the smell. Do they smell more keenly than mine, I wondered? Then suddenly I knew that they didn't. I was riddled with this extraordinary scent, moist and heavy, like a thousand autumns, acres of hay longing to be cut. I stared for a long time before walking to the house.

4

My garden curved, like a segment of fruit or a half-moon, from the gate to the front door. The house itself was square. It had been built in the days when houses were getting rarer and the ones that were built assumed ever-more-manageable forms. I walked through that curve of garden, past our roses, carrying that strange new sensation. I stopped then, just beyond the roses. I became conscious of a sound. It was a whispering, liquid and lispish, and it grew. I was carrying a briefcase, as I always do. I looked down to my left. All the gardens seemed to sing at once, a symmetrical hum of praise to that afternoon that would have been forgotten by anyone but me, and even by me, had the thing not begun. They curved away out of my vision and I imagined the last garden overhanging the sea, the same dullish hot blue that it had been for months, ivy trailing down a broken brick wall and touching the glimmering water. There must be a reason, I thought, the gardens are opening their pores. Then I walked towards the glass door, realising that the smell was cut grass and the sound was the hissing of sprinklers.

3

Of course I wondered would Marianne's friends be there, talking about the heat, about the weather. I would not have been surprised to see, through the hallway and the open living-room door, the Ambroses sitting round our glass-topped table drinking weak coffee from our long, thin cups. I would have said something inconsequential I suppose, and retreated to the conservatory to think. There I could look out on the back garden and watch the shadow creep round the sundial, the broad leaves of the knee-high grass glistening in the hot light, the garden which was by now a whispering, torrid tangle of olive-green. I could think there about the changes, without panic or despair.

But there were no Ambroses and Marianne was standing alone in the dark of the hallway. She glanced up when I came in and mouthed my name with that slight diffidence in her voice which was by now familiar to me. There had once been nothing diffident in our love. Her red hair was falling around the nape of her neck, so white that it always reminded me of china. She was turning and turning on her finger her band of gold.

Matilde is sick, she said.

I touched her neck, where the hair curled round it. She withdrew slightly, and shivered.

She's been calling for you.

Marianne walked through to the living-room. I turned upstairs and saw my fleeting shape in the mirror over the first steps. I stopped and walked back down. That shadow had for some reason disturbed me. I saw my shoulder enter the left-hand corner of the mirror and stared. I hardly recognised the stranger who stared back at me. Had I not looked for so long, I wondered. I stared for a long while and concluded that I mustn't have. Certain moods of self-loathing had in the past kept me from mirrors, but never had the gap between what I remembered and what I eventually saw been so large. Marianne moved into the living-room. Matilde called my name. I left my image then, carried on up the stairs and into her room.

Matilde lay curled on the bed, her hair tracing the curve of her child's back. I touched her forehead and felt the heat there. She turned and looked at me, her eyelids seemed heavy with the weight of her long lashes. The almond green of her eyes was flecked with gold. They stared at me, knowing more about myself than I ever could. She lifted her head slightly and her lips brushed the hairs on the back of my fingers.

I was dreaming of you, she murmured.

She seemed not yet out of sleep, or feverish. I could see my reflection in her pupil, ringed and flecked with almond. I was curved there, my cheekbones and forehead were large, the rest of me retreating into the darkness of her gaze.

Read me a story.

The stories she favoured were of unicorns and mythical beasts. She would drink in every detail of those creatures, the bulging arch of their brow, the skull the skin of

7

which is so thick it could have been scaled, the luxuriant hair along each arm and palm of hand. So I read once more of the merchant with the three daughters, the sunken ship, the sea journey to the garden and the waiting beast.

After a while her eyes closed and her breathing became a long slow murmur and the blush on her forehead faded a little. I looked out through her window and saw the sun had vanished from the fronds of grass. I made my way out there and listened to the hissing of sprinklers from neighbouring lawns. I could see the mauve haze descend on the town, somewhere beyond my garden. There was the hum of night machines beginning, taking over from the last roars of day. I touched my finger off the sundial, so hot with the day's sun that it burnt the skin. I rubbed the burnt spot, noticing how hard it was. I rubbed finger after finger then and found each of them hard. Again I wondered how long since I had done this, or had this leathern hardness suddenly appeared? I looked around for no reason other than impulse and saw Marianne in the kitchen window, staring at me. I saw what she saw then, which was me, hunched and predatory, bending over a sundial to stare back at her. Her red hair glistened and her eyes shone. I shambled towards her through olive-green growth. There was the smell of burnt meat.

The radio was crackling when I went in. Let me help you, I said to her. I took the hot plates from the oven. Again my flesh stuck to the surface, but I felt even less than before. The meat was smoking gently and the smell of flesh drifted round the room. Sit down, I said to her. The word love, which I wanted to utter, froze on my lips. When I touched her neck, just where the red hair met the white, she pulled back sharply from my hand.

We ate the vegetables first and then the meat. The voice on the radio crackled on, bringing as it always did the slight panic of the outside world. Turn it off, I asked Marianne, but she didn't want to and so it drifted on like a voice between us, making our conversation for us. What is happening, I asked her after a while. I don't know, she answered.

While I washed the things, I heard her inside, tinkering on the bass notes of the piano. It was quite late by then, since we always ate late. I walked from the kitchen into the living-room. Can I play with you, I asked her.

She made room for me around the higher notes. We played the Chaconne in D minor, in a duet form we had worked out in the first months of our love. She played the bass as smoothly as ever, almost without a thought. My fingers found it hard to stretch, though, and an awkward rhythm crept into the tune. She was annoyed, understandably. She stood up swiftly after the end of the tune and lit a cigarette. I stared at my fingers, which were still holding the white keys. I heard the note hang in the air long after it should have died. Will you come to bed, Marianne asked me.

We made love of course. I watched her undress and thought of all the words to do with this activity. My mind soon exhausted itself. I took her white throwaway pants in my fingers. She was lying under the featherdown sheet waiting for me. She turned off the light. I buried my face in her paper pants, then took off my own clothes.

There is a halo round you, she said. I looked down at myself. There was light coming through the window. Each hair on my body seemed isolated by that light like a bluish gossamer, a wrapping. It is a trick of the light, I thought. I made my way to the bed and felt her hand reaching out for mine. It rested on my arms.

Her fingers were long and bony, but soft, with the softness of her white neck. I had known them in so many ways, clutching the pillow, rubbing my cheek, scouring my back, that the fact that they felt different now didn't seem remarkable. Something was happening, I knew, with us as well as with the rest of it. She ran them down my arms and all the small hairs there sprang to attention. I touched her eyes with my fingers, which miraculously seemed to have lost all their hardness, they were like pads, responsive to her every pore. Her eyelids fluttered beneath them and so I drew my fingers down her cheeks to the bone of her jaw and down to that white neck. I leaned my face forwards and kissed her lips. My mouth seemed larger than human, able to protect hers in its clasp. I felt her tongue beating against my lips and opened them and soon I felt her saliva in mine. My mouth crawled down her body and she opened her vagina for me. Her murmurs seemed to fill the air. Her knees were bent around the small curve at the back of my head, pressing it downwards. We seemed to twine round each other as if our limbs had lost their usual shape. We made the beast with two backs then and somewhere in between our cries another cry was heard, a little more urgent. Matilde was standing in the doorway, still in her dream.

You go to her, Marianne said, turning over. I rose from the bed and took her in my arms, which seemed no longer pliant, but heavy and cumbersome in every movement. Matilde whispered parts of her dream to me as I carried her to bed.

Marianne was asleep when I got back. I looked at my body in the dark and saw all the tiny hairs glistening in

10

the moonlight. I began to dream, standing there. There was a skylight and the moon in my bedroom shifted above me, for I was a child, with face pressed to the skylight, staring down below. There were women, crossing and recrossing a parquet floor. Each woman carried a cup. The cups glistened with liquid. They entered a tiny arch and came out again with each cup empty. I inched my way down the glass to see better and for the first time noticed my shadow below, marked-out by the moon, much larger than I was. They noticed it too, for they all pressed into a circle and stared at me together, their raised faces like a large ageing daisy. The glass below me melted slowly and they each held a cup up to catch the drops. I melted in turn and an arm gathered me in a raised cup and a woman's face with two soft, feathered lips bent towards me to drink.

I awoke and the moon was outside the gauze curtain once more and Marianne was beside me, a swathe of crumpled blanket between us. Her slightly tilted nose and her upper lip jutting out from her lower looked strange, strange because once so familiar. How I would dream when we first met of that full petulant rose of her upper lip, the dreaming wistfulness it gave to her face. I would try to describe it in words, as if talking to a stranger. But no stranger could have understood.

I touched her long athlete's back and she shivered in her sleep, drew the sheets around her. She pulled away as if from a stranger. I looked at my hand on the white sheet that covered her white skin. It was much darker than it should have been. The skin was wrinkled and glistening, like the soft pad that is underneath a dog's paw. The nails were hard, thicker than they had been in the afternoon, the points curling round the tips of the

11

fingers. There were five blisters there, from the burning of the sundial and the hot plates. I covered my hand with what was left of my end of the sheet and lay with my mouth close as it could be to her hair without waking her, my breath shifting the strands at ever longer intervals as sleep overtook me.

4

When I awoke the sun was coming through the gauze curtains, cutting the air in two with a beam that hit the edges of the sheet wrapped round my legs. The dust wheeled in the beam towards the green carpeted floor. I heard the sound of the front door closing and of Matilde making her way towards school. There was the sound of clattering dishes and of the lawn sprinklers starting on their circular motion. Marianne came down the corridor and as she neared the room I wrapped myself in the sheet as a cover. I saw her in the mirror when she entered and she must have caught my glance for she turned and told me in that soft brusque voice that it was late. When she left the room again I rose. I kept my eyes from my body since sunlight is so much more revealing than nightlight. Both hands fitted through my shirtsleeves only with extreme difficulty. I dressed fully and slowly and made my way to the kitchen.

The moods that were between us were almost richer than speech. I sat watching her eat, eating only occasionally myself. However much I loved to watch her, I knew there was nothing I could do to dispel this silence. It had its roots in things done and said and it was like ivy now, twining round me. I spoke a few words, but my voice sounded harsh and unnatural. I then rose to leave and tucked my hands round my leather case, walking backwards towards the door. She told me that the Ambroses would be dinner-guests tonight. I will come home early, I said, and talk to you. There's something I must say. Do, she answered.

But what had it been that I had intended to say, I wondered, when I passed through the gate and began the walk down the long sequence of lawns. The heat had brought a mist from over the waters, it clung to the edges of the lawns and the grass borders of the pavement. There was a steady movement of people from the lawns, down the pavement, towards the city.

The sea glistened from beneath the mists and I left the crowds waiting for the trains which I knew might never appear and walked along the tracks. Wisps of haze clung to the sleepers. I walked calmly, but inside me was building an unreasonable joy. This joy was nameless, seemed to come from nowhere, but I found if I gave my thoughts to it it answered back, asking nothing of me. It frothed inside me. The leather of my briefcase seemed moulded to my palm. I brushed back my hair. My tough nails scraped off my forehead and my hair leapt apart at the bidding of my fingers. The joy abated then and became still water. I knew I must keep it as much a secret as my monstrous hands. I heard a sound behind me and leapt back as a train thundered past.

I walked through the smoking piles on the outskirts of the city till the tracks tunnelled beneath the ground. I let the sleepers guide me through the void. I emerged in a long corridor of glass with listless crowds below, waiting for trains. I made my way to the silver escalator, which had been still for some years now.

In Nassau Street the tendrils of plants swung over the

14

railings and brushed off the crumbling brickwork. The gaps between buildings gave a view of clear blue sky. The haze was dispersing now. I knew Morgan would be sitting in the office we shared, with his green eyeshade jutting from his forehead, his sharp observant eyes fixed on the drawing-board. I feared what those eyes would notice and so stopped off at a tailor's shop. I bought a pair of gloves, there, several sizes too big for what I once had been. I fitted them on behind a tailor's dummy while the assistant busied himself with labels. They made two large white, knotted lumps of my hands, more noticeable to me, I hoped, than to anyone else.

I reached our office in Crow Street. There was a games parlour downstairs that opened out onto the street. I saw the screens glowing dimly inside, lit every now and then with flashes of white, the shadows of youths bent over them. I made my way upstairs to where Morgan sat, his eyeshade cutting his face with a half-moon of green.

Having been partners for years, we talked very little. Whether we didn't need to or didn't want to had become unimportant, since it was comforting just to know each other's movements, to be allowed room in another's presence, to work in alternative rooms and make coffee on alternate days. We liked each other, and I rarely heard Morgan complain about the heat. From his window he could see the wide street spill over to the giant building opposite where the paper-sellers would crowd with each new edition calling the days' news. He would talk about the quality of coffee I made, about the crossword puzzles and the state of trains, but he would never question, senses of panic and unease were unknown to him. He did the elevations, the line-drawings, the

15

fine-pencilled work. I would do the colours, the story-boards, the broad sketches.

He told me a woman had called, and would call again later. I walked past him and picked up, besides the acrid smell of his sharpened pencils, the smell of something quite different. As I entered my room it seemed to follow me, or I followed it. I knew that smell, though I hadn't met it before.

I had been given details over the phone. She represented a perfume firm who wanted to advertise a thing called musk. She had described the associations she wanted the odour to carry in the minds of the public. It was to be feminine, seductive, yet to carry a hint of threat, like an aroused woman surrounded by a threat she cannot touch, feel or even see. So I had sketched a long rectangular drawing, almost Cinemascope in shape. On the left-hand side was a white, porcelain bath. There were ornate brass taps, a female leg crooked between them, dangling over the floor, the rest of the body beyond the picture's confines. A fine-boned hand was soaping the leg. Water trickled over the arch of the foot and gathered in drops at the perfect heel. The floor was patterned in black and white tiles, of which I'd forced the perspective a little, so the lines seemed to run like a web to the farthest wall. The dripping water from heel to floor then carried your eye over the chequerboard tiles to an open door and a corridor outside. On the open door was a gilt mirror. Full-length, turned in such a way that the bather couldn't see it, it reflected the corridor outside. And there I had sketched in a marble table, a telephone, a discarded bathrobe just thrown on the carpeted floor. There was an empty space, in the vague outline of a figure. That was to be the threat, awaiting definition.

It was odd to see my work on the boards, a product of yesterday's thoughts. I was different now, and found myself looking at it with a certain nostalgia. That threat, which seemed to be one thing yesterday, would be quite another today. I took my pen in my swollen hands and began to draw. Soon the pain of bending my massive fingers eased and the lines came. The lines of that fallen bathrobe seemed to clash with anything vertical and so I knew he would be prone, whatever else he was. I lined in a sinuous passive object almost touching the robe. The shape became bunched like a fist and the nails sunk into the carpet went deep, like claws. Hardly human, the curves of that bunched fist went backwards, always close to the floor, more a stretching leg than an arm. It began to rise then, with all the majesty and sureness of a sphinx. There was a torso there, waiting to emerge. I sat there, feeling it grow. It was all sensation, no line could have drawn its image. My back rippled and arched, there was a scent everywhere. There was the sound of a door opening.

She was wearing a hat, with a black fringe of lace round it. There was a small smile on her lips which showed that one upper tooth was cracked and angled inwards slightly. She walked slowly through the room, leaving that scent in the air behind her. I stayed at my board with my pen in my hands and my hands between my knees. I glanced at her every now and then. She had mumbled a word or two of greeting, hardly listening for an answer. She traced an arc round my things, picking up a sketch here and there and an odd finished drawing, the way professionals do, tilting her head as if to assess it, but already I knew her interest was more than professional. I find it difficult to explain how I knew this; my hands

17

began to feel damp, as if they were sweating copiously under the bandages. Most of all it was the scent, which seemed to hang in the air like figures of eight. I felt that creature in my drawing in the empty shape in the corridor begin to grow, like a growing-pain. I could not yet see the form it would take, but I knew now that I would recognise it when it came, as I recognised that scent, which carried the name musk.

She pulled over the swivel chair and sat down beside me.

This is it, then, she said, looking at my drawing.

I said it was as yet only an idea. My voice sounded strange to me. Not so much hoarse as furred. I told myself I should not be embarrassed. But that scent, when she was close, was overpowering.

We need something extraordinary, she whispered. Things are so bad, firms are on the line. They want me to bring them a miracle.

I said nothing. I was a professional after all, not a miracle-worker. But I felt the pressure of something extraordinary, too extraordinary to be talked of. I felt a throbbing, like a pain, in my back, beginning in my left shoulder-blade, then creeping its way round my ribs. There was a knot of fur in my throat.

She changed from talk of the picture to talk of herself. I listened while she told her story. She came from the country intending to be a nurse but found all the hospitals overstaffed. I could see what a wonderful nurse she would have made. She had beautifully long bones in her arms and hands that folded with this restfulness. Her hair was auburn under the black lace and would have swung around her face as she bent over each bed and, together with those hands, would have given the bandaged heads a sense of heavenly reassurance. She told me how she wandered from job to job, mostly on the fringes of artistic worlds. Her tall figure and her auburn hair were considered a suitable adjunct to galleries and theatre foyers. She felt outside the events that went on there and yet people seemed to think, she told me, that she embodied their essence. Her present job had been foisted upon her out of the same misapprehension.

She had finished her story. Her odalisque eyes were wide open on mine all the time she spoke. They were by no means beautiful, but they gripped me. I fell into the dream again, with the daylight all around me, I saw a long, golden stretch of desert. Nothing moved except occasional flurries of sand which rose in tiny whorls, as if filling vacuums in the air. The sand was sculpted in hillocks, which could have been the length of miles or the length of a fingernail. My eyes sped over these stretches, the outlines hardly varying till the expanse was broken by a jagged rectangular shape, pure black, sinking at an angle into the sand. It was marble, porphyry, or some alloy of glass. Inside I could glimpse a face, barely visible in that blackness of ice, hair frozen in statuesque, perpetual disarray. I had never seen the face before. One of the teeth was cracked.

She saw the half-drawn shape by the bathrobe as some kind of beast. I told her that was the obvious form for such a threat to take, but what kind of beast? She mused about it for a while, and began to enumerate species. I stopped her, telling her it was unwise to presume, one must let it assume a form of its own, one that we could never anticipate. She suggested a visit to the zoo tomorrow, to muse further. I agreed. She left then, tipping my arm every so slightly, as if to impart some hidden message, or to imply some secret we shared.

I drew a few more lines. Soon my arms became extra-ordinarily heavy. My head was swimming with images. I let the pencil fall, let my arms hang by my sides and breathed deeply. Slowly and inexorably, the rush of joy built up. It was like a gathering wind. I sat there with my back slightly bent, my hands dangling and swinging gently as if to the sound of late afternoon traffic outside, the smell of musk in the air. The windows were rattling with the wind and beneath all sounds I could hear the deepest one, the one that was at the base of all sounds. I had never heard it before, but recognised it instantly. It came from below the building, from the earth itself. As if the roots of being stretched down, so deep down like a tuning-fork, and sang with an eternal hum.

Morgan must have come in then, for my interest was diverted and the joy slowly subsided. He had taken off his eyeshade, the first of the signals of his imminent return home. I rose from my chair. My arms felt light once more. Outside, night was coming down on the full street.

5

✄✄✄✄✄✄

Night had begun to fall with a disturbing swiftness. Without any of the change from summer to autumn, around 1800 the sky would begin its wheel from cobalt to blue, and down in the streets faces, buildings and vegetable growths would be lit with a strange, lurid glare. It was the glare of changing, of heightened shadows, it threw darkened shadows under the eyes of passers-by. There was this yellow, febrile glow until the night lights took over.

The hot air seemed to enclose the crowds in a continuous bubble of movement. They arched their bodies, embraced, queued, made talk and love against the peeling brick. They seemed to glory, for a few brief moments, in the heat, in the sense of lost time and future. Their brightly coloured shirts and skirts moved towards me, the women indistinguishable from the men.

Morgan turned left at the river. I could see the bands of youths gathered outside the game halls. I could hear the buzzing of innumerable machines. I crossed the bridge. The crowds always seemed about to engulf me but clove apart as I approached. I suddenly felt older than any of them, older than anyone I could possibly have met. My steps became halting, my neck scraped off the collar of my suit with the roughness of what felt again like the pad beneath a dog's paw.

I found myself outside the station. The artificial palm fronds which passed me on the escalator seemed limp with the day's heat. Inside on the platform the crowds were there again, waiting for the train's arrival. The eaves on the corridor of glass above each held a drop of moisture which grew to fullness only to fall and be imperceptibly replaced by another. It seemed so much like rain, but I knew that to be an impossibility. And sure enough I saw a man in a blue uniform standing between the tracks holding the nozzle of a hose and sending a high arc of spray over the glass skylight and the artificial fronds alike. Walking on sleepers when the light is gone is foolhardy, I knew, so I stood in the shadows waiting for the train. The spray cleared the grime from the glass above and made the light and shade harsher. The man walked past me with his arc of water, dragging the pipe behind him in an arc of black.

The hall filled up with steam then and glass was obscured by billows of smoke behind which liquid flashes still managed to glint. In the shadows of the palm frond I rubbed my cheek with my left hand. I saw a series of tiny flakes twirl towards the ground, displaying a rainbow of colours in the half-light. I saw the crowds press from the platform into bunches round each door. I moved out from the shadows and pressed my way amongst them. I held my face down. I was disturbed at the thought of what it might reveal to them. Knowing how each one of us assumes that what is seen of him by others is not what he knows to be the truth but a mask, I felt a sudden terror that the whole of me was about to be laid bare. Whatever adjunct of our persons it is that maintains this demeanour, it was slowly leaving me, I realised that now. The skin of my person was being shed to usher in a new season, a new age. It would peel off me slowly and inexorably as if pulled by a giant hand.

My main concern, though, was that others should not see what I knew now to be the case. I pressed myself behind the last backs at the door nearest to me. I have always been considerate of others. My urge to spare their feelings will drive me to outlandish lengths. So I took my place some distance from the doorway, my face to the wall. When the train lurched forwards, our bodies swung to one side, then the other. The last of the evening light bled in both windows.

The movement slowly lulled us all. I felt the cramped space between windows easing a little. I let my eyes take in the shapes around me. Bowed shoulders and heads led in waves to the window opposite. The angular city drifted by the glass, then gave way to the tips and heads of the outskirts and behind them a steady thread of blue sea. This blue slowly came to fill the window and to outline, and darken by contrast, the face that was nearest it. It belonged to an ageing lady. She had cascades of lines round her eyes and a fullness round the cheekbones that softened these with warmth. As the blue sea faded from the window a white, rich light slowly filled her face. She was remembering, I sensed. Her eyes were creased with those tiny wrinkles and had the wistfulness of everything that is best in humans. I knew I would either meet her again, or had seen her before. Then slowly recognition dawned. She was my mother.

6

※※※※※※

I twisted my body so I faced the opposite window. I heard a loud rending sound and several heads turned. I kept my face down, but from the corner of my eye could see that she had noticed nothing, she was in a world of remembrance all of her own. I remembered the poplar trees at the end of our garden and the plaid rug she spread beneath me. I looked down at my right arm and then my left. My sleeve had split below the elbow and the bandage was now in shreds. The change had spread to my wrist and then must have raced in a sudden surge towards the knot of muscle in my forearm. She would roll up the sleeves of her dress to let me count the freckles on her skin. I knew she lived upon the route but had never seen her take the train before. I would count the freckles till my eyes swam. My weekly visits had become an embarrassment of late with the gloom that swept over me in waves. I thought of how she must have missed me. In one full moment I felt how much I had missed her. My longing to touch her seemed to fill the carriage like a soaking cloud, like steam. A strange warmth rose from the whole of my body. I felt a dry rustle on my forearms and heard a soft fall on the floor, as if innumerable flakes were drifting downwards. I imagined them on the metal, in an untidy pile. They would be swept away on the

24

return journey, perhaps by that porter with the water-spray. He would drown these shards of me without a thought.

I saw my mother's expression changing. From her window she could obviously see the platform approaching. The train halted and she left, with several others. There was more room, but I stayed pressed in the shadows. I imagined her walking down the blue-lit street towards the house I grew up in. I wondered would the time ever be right to call. I suspected it might not be.

My platform crept through that window, the train halted, I walked up the concrete steps. The liquid blue lay like a shroud over the tracks, the undergrowth beyond them and the rows of houses above. I walked, trailing my torn sleeve and bandage behind me.

The sprinklers were uttering their last whispers. Small piles of grass lay gathered beneath each rosebush. A dog barked from the third garden. A door opened and then closed again. I saw a car outside our house, with sounds coming from it. They were bright, chattering voices, so brisk and hopeful that for a moment I imagined they belonged to the Ambroses themselves. But as I drew nearer I heard the metallic crackles of the airwaves and saw the red light of the radio flashing on the dashboard.

7

❧❧❧❧❧

The front door was open. I heard voices coming from the kitchen. I walked quietly past, up the stairs and into the bathroom. My cheeks had begun to discolour in blotches, the skin ridged and bumped along them, puckered with holes. I put plasters over each one and I wrapped a long white bandage over my forearm, which was by now unrecognisable. Everything had changed or would change, I knew, and this knowledge made my efforts to hide it even more pathetic, and yet I pressed on with them. Such is the persistence of the human, I thought, and made my way downstairs again.

The voices seemed involved, like those on the car radio, in some common human drama. James's was the loudest and yet I could not distinguish the words. I heard a sound that was like an insect's hum for his, with an odd, irregular climax. I heard a more plaintive note for Marianne. Mary's sound I could not hear at all. I saw all three of them turning towards me when I entered. James rose and the hum became more and more irregular as if the insect was beating its wings fiercely, to escape. I avoided shaking his hand. I noticed for the first time how awkward his bones were, how he was all bumps and angles under his sleek black suit. His temple lobes were too long and his nose too sharp. Mary turned and smiled

26

but her eyes were wide open in a stare that seemed as if it would never lose its amazement. Her pupils throbbed with the beating of her heart. Marianne looked up momentarily and smiled. Then the fringe of her hair covered her face as she held out a plate to me.

I heard all three sounds start at once, in conversation. There was tongue on the plate before me. I ate slowly, something of the flavour of the creature disagreed with me. James's hum throbbed on, swinging round towards me now and then like a pendulum. I heard the sound of Marianne's voice answering for me. It was soft, conch-like, falling like a wave, as if to protect me. I continued to eat. The soft threads of tongue on my own tongue made me feel as if somehow what I ate was myself. I looked up and saw Mary's eyes fall.

James hummed and rose an interval or two, then soared up an octave. Was it because I could not distinguish the words that I felt the need to talk? Or did his tone enrage me to the point of utterance? I knew I had embarrassed them, I knew it was all wrong, but I felt the need to tell them about the joy. You could not believe the joy of what has happened, I said to them, though everything may point to its opposite. Let me describe to you that unreasonable beauty that fills up my soul, unreasonable only because so unexpected . . .

I stopped when I saw my words were not helping any. There was absolute silence for a moment, then the sound of the tongue on James's plate being rent and lifted to his mouth. Then the sounds of conversation began again. They were coloured this time with a deep blush, as if with shame for something that had happened.

I rose with difficulty and excused myself. I crossed the

27

long distance to the living-room door. The silence kept on. I closed the door behind me then and made my way across the hallway. I could hear the sounds raising themselves again. I went into the music-room. I looked at my bandages, which were now stained in places with a dull, rust-coloured liquid. I suspected I was sweating. I sat down at the piano and began to play. Though my fingers were cramped by the swathes I did get through, slowly and haltingly, the first part of the Chaconne. The long, full bass notes seemed to throb through the piano's frame, to mine, to the floor itself. I thought of the question, as I played, of why music soothes the restless soul.

I heard the sound of voices at the doorway, then Marianne's footsteps back along the hall and the sound of a dinner evening ending. I stopped, I had lost the urge to play. I saw the liquid had seeped from my fingers on to the keys, staining the white ones with irregular threads. It made highlights on the black ones too. It looked like weakened syrup, but I suspected it might taste of salt. It was not at all unpleasant. I heard Marianne's footsteps up the stairway and the sound then of large, heavy rustling from upstairs. I followed, soon after.

The weight of my form must have shifted towards my head and torso, for walking up the stairs I had to grab the rails every now and then to stop myself falling backwards. The house was silent now but for a rustling of bedclothes somewhere and the tiny hum of Matilde's breath. I stood on the landing, listening to the new quality of this silence. Slowly it came to me that silence was not what for years I had supposed it to be, the absence of sound. It was the absence, I knew now, of the foreground sounds so the background sounds could be heard. These sounds were like breath – like the breath of this house, of the movement of the air inside it, of the creatures who lived in it. They seemed to wheel around me till I heard a piece of furniture being pulled somewhere, too much in the foreground, and the spell was dispersed.

I knew I must wash myself before the next move. Now was not the time to approach Marianne, and when that time came cleanliness would be essential. The bathroom, like that of most of our neighbours, was our pride and joy. The taps were gleaming silver, with handles and spigots elaborately wrought, with an elegant adjustable arm fixed to one side, holding a shower nozzle. The spray that came from this was fine and hard, with a lever at its base which changed the water gradually from cold to the sharpest heat. I thought of the countless times I had stood beneath it, in a different season, and the water had stroked me with its heat, washed away all the grass cuttings till Marianne sometimes joined me, her hair bundled beneath a cellophane cap, closing her eyes with pleasure and pain at the heat and her mouth puckering as she did so, waiting to be kissed. I would kiss her and let the water palm us both and her eyes would open as much as they could under the streams, her spare lashes looking like drowned kittens, her fingers, each one, edged into the ribs on my sides. The kiss would last until the hot water ran out and it would be a test of each other's endurance to wait through the cold till it came back, for the heat came in cycles.

So I remembered as I undid my hands how it was she who taught me to be excessively clean and how there are some lessons one should never unlearn. Now my hand was not my own, I saw the ridges and tufts of flesh come

29

clear of the bandages, the hair matted with liquid and the muscles like scallops leading up to the forearm. I peeled off the other hand and the rest of my sodden clothes and ran the bath as I did so. The shower water would be riddled with memories; I thought I was wise to bathe in preference but discovered my mistake when the enamel filled enough to still the liquid and my reflection became clear. I had come to accept that I was not myself but had no conception of the enormity of the disparity between me and the being who confronted me. He was arresting, without a doubt, his forehead was tall, his nose broad and somewhat pushed in as if some afternoon, years ago, it had been broken in a fall. His hair was luxuriant and thick and swept back in clumps from his crown. His eyes were almond-shaped, fronted by even bushes of hair, white round the edges of the almond, streaked a little with red, then amber, gathering into black. Beneath his neck, which was ridged with two angular tendons, was a sharp V, then a scalloped expanse which swept in sharply then to his stomach which in turn swept in towards a tiny whorl. Beyond his stomach my vision was blocked by the edge of the bath but that was enough to see what a piece of work I had become. I stepped into the steaming water and dispelled my image with ripples. I found my changeable limbs floated with a strange bouy-ancy and took no stock at all of the heat. It filled them with ease, dispersed all thoughts of strangeness from me, everything found its place. How natural it seemed to loll in that water, to turn and face the air again and turn again. The steam rose in the darkness like versions of myself and the lapping water seemed to echo round the lawns. I held it in my monstrous hands and let it drip down to the whorl on my stomach, where it gathered till it spilled over my flat sides. I couldn't have noticed the door opening, for I saw a shape in the corner of my vision then, a white shape, and it seemed to have been there some time. It was Matilde, in her nightgown. By her wide-open eyes, I knew she was still in her dream. Her dreams of beasts were never nightmares, for her stare had all the fascination of a child for an object of wonder. Her eyes travelled down the length of this body that jutted in and out of water, that filled her dream, that perhaps even was her dream. A knotted hand clutched the edge of the bath and she blew soft air out of her lips to ruffle it. I raised both hands and turned her then in the direction of the door. She walked out that way as silently as she had come.

I heard the rustle of her bedclothes and her turning over to sleep. I raised myself from the water and hammered the bath with the droplets that fell from me. I searched for a towel in the dark, but could not find one. I walked outside into the hallway and lay down in the thick carpet, letting it absorb the moisture. I turned on my back, then on my front, stared back towards the bathroom door. It was open. The gilt mirror fixed to the doorway held the reflection of the bath, but none of myself.

Within minutes I was dry. I rose and walked down towards the bedroom. The corridor seemed shrunk, as if the angles had become forced in upon each other. Through the bedroom door I could see the moon behind the gauze curtains. Marianne was asleep on the bed, the blankets rolled tightly about her. She had thrown two blankets on to the floor at her feet. I reached out my hand to touch her shoulder, but saw its texture against her white skin and withdrew it again. I rolled myself in the blankets at her feet.

8

When I awoke Marianne was above me. She had thrown more blankets down, whether because of the excessive heat, or from the impulse to cover my shape, I tried not think. I had all the appearance of sleep and so didn't move when she threw one leg over my shoulder to stretch for her stockings. I watched her cover herself with pants and then sheath each leg with nylon and saw her breasts vanish under a brassiere. She raised both hands in the air and drew on a flower-patterned blouse. She slipped her feet into two white high-heeled shoes, then drew her heels back sharply, grazing my cheek with a metal tip. She wrapped a kilt around her and walked from the room.

I lay on. I had awoken, but my dream was still with me. The moon shone through opulent French windows on to a parquet floor. The resinous gleam from the floor was similar to that over which the women had traced their circles. I was suspended from above, swinging inches above that gleam. The hairs of my cheeks brushed off the varnish. My eyes followed the rope which bound me, a vertical climb up to a creaking pulley, then a long sagging angle away. My eyes followed the rope down that angle to the floor, where it was knotted round the heel of a high-heeled shoe. There was a leg in the shoe which gave it weight and substance, immensity even, and yet strangely fine proportions with its line of ankle moving smoothly to the swell of calf. I swung my body on the rope. I rocked myself in ever-widening arcs towards that heel. I held out my arms to grip at the ankle but could never quite reach. Then the foot walked off abruptly, as if its owner was tired of waiting. I was swept quickly to the ceiling. I shattered the skylight through to the moon.

Marianne came in again. She unwrapped the tartan kilt from around herself and pulled on a skirt instead. When she had gone, I pulled the blankets down. My body responded only slowly to my efforts to move. My veins seemed sluggish and all my muscles seemed grossly overstretched. I made it over to the wardrobe and sought out my largest suit. This was a dress-suit, with adjustable buttons for waistcoat, jacket and trousers. I found a white starched shirt-front which I tied around my neck, since none of my shirts, I knew, would cover me. The problem of shoes I solved by slitting the sides so wide that my feet could splay through the opening. I then tore one shirt into strips for use as bandages, since my stock had quite run out. I waited then till I heard Matilde leave for school, then made my way downstairs.

Marianne was sitting with her face to the window. There was coffee across the table from her, with a bowl for me. I sat and ate as quietly as possible. She didn't turn or speak. Her red hair fell away in strands from her cheek-bones. Her mouth expressed both hurt and horror, but most of all a kind of outrage. When I had finished the bowl I got up to leave. She turned her face towards me as I was at the door. There were tears rolling down each cheek.

She asked me how I could do this to her. I replied that

33

it was not me that was doing it. Again the sound of my voice made me not want to say anything further. She said she would like to kiss me, but could not bring herself to. Will I kiss you then, I asked. When she nodded, I walked towards her. My shadow reached her first. I bent down and brought my lips to her cheek. Her tears moistened my lips and brought them some relief. I stood up then and thanked her, and made my way to the door. I didn't look back.

Such is the complexity of the human, I thought, as I made my way to the station. My appearance attracted attention, but I kept my eyes rigidly ahead. Anger, pity, love, hate, the names we give to our emotions signify a separateness, a purity that is rarely in fact the case. She had stared with anger, pity, love and hate. I walked, again, along the buckling tracks. The sea was leaden today, like a pit of salt, with only a little mist. The fronds of the artificial palms, when I came to them, were still fresh and erect after their night watering. Morgan's eye-shades touched the drawing-board in greeting when I entered.

I sat down to work. I began with tiny details, put the major questions quite out of my mind, and as often happens when that is the case, the details themselves began to answer the questions. I filled in the high-lights and shadows of the enamel bath. This led me to her leg, which I lit with an almost porcelain finish. The shadow fell from an unseen light-source, cutting an angle between the side of the bath and the carpeted floor. I followed the tuft of carpet the way one does a wheat-field, with a series of vertical strokes nearest the eye, followed by a ruffled expanse. The sun was falling on the left-hand side of my face. I rubbed my cheek occasionally, because of the itching of the heat, causing a shower of flakes to litter the page, which I each time duly blew away. And in this way I was led to the figure. He extended himself from the tufts of carpet, with a shape that was indeed sphinxlike, two noble paws pressed deep into the pile. Sphinx though seemed too common a name for the creature he was becoming. I teased my mind as I drew with names for him, but any others that occurred seemed equally inadequate.

I had him half-sketched when I suddenly broke off. I found myself exhausted without knowing how or why. The sun had nearly crossed my drawing board which was, I surmised, more than two hours' journey. I remembered my appointment. I rubbed my face and snowed the drawing once more. I went to Morgan's room, but he was out. His room was eerily silent, as if he had never been there. I decided to walk.

I wrapped my bandages round my hands, arranged my shirt-front so it covered the widest possible area and ruffled any further flakes from my hair and face. I then borrowed Morgan's eyeshade, the shadow of which I hoped would be more than enough to cover my visage. Then I ventured out.

9

How long was it since I had walked between morning and night? The city seemed to curl under the sun like a scalded leech. The shadows were tall and black, the pavements white and empty. I crossed Westmoreland Street alone, the only movement the rustling in the patches under the walls. Is the world to be left to me, I wondered, and such as me? A statue of hot bronze pointed nowhere, his finger warped by the years of sunshine. I walked through the sleeping city, blinded by the glare, meeting no one. I came to the river, which had narrowed to a trickle in its caked bed. I walked beside it up by Parkgate Street. The Wellington Monument jabbed towards the white haze, I passed through the parched Hollow towards that long avenue, whose perspectives seemed to beckon towards splendours unseen. I saw then, after some time, a shape approaching out of the melting tarmac. I heard the clip-clop of hooves and readied myself to spring into the bushes, in case I met horse and rider. But no, it was a deer which walked down towards me and stopped some feet away, as I did, to stare. I noted the grace of his rectangular jaw, the dapples that led from it to his sprouting horns. Do you see things differently from me, I felt like asking, are your perspectives wider than mine, have you two planes of vision to carry everywhere you go? Whether I thought this or phrased it, he seemed to hear, for his lower jaw moved at odds with his upper and he bounded past me, in two neat, langorous leaps, as if inviting me to imitate him. I merely watched him, though, disappear into the city haze.

As I walked on, the shape in front of me defined itself. I could see a glittering white façade with two proud pillars and the whorling fingers of a wrought-iron gate between. Walking further, more pillars defined themselves, white ones, stretching in pleasing harmonies from the façade of the house. It slowly dawned on me that it was the presidential palace. Then the memories came. They flooded in on me, like the dreams, the avenue was full of them. I leaned against a slim tall tree, with no foliage at all except for an umbrella at the top. I saw my mother, walking towards it. She was wearing a narrow pleated jacket, with a flowered skirt. She was walking down the avenue, holding my hand. I was pulling her towards the hedge beyond. She wished to view the palace from behind the gates, but I wanted to see – what was it I wanted to see? The zoo, I realised. And I stepped out from under my tree-trunk, remembering. Enclosed by those hedges, I remembered, the animals would leap at that tall barbed wire, lining the path to the presidential palace.

I crossed the avenue and walked along the hedge. I heard a few mournful snarls, as if of creatures woken for the first time in years. I came to a turnstile and walked through. The Swiss-style cottage was still there, but now it gave out no afternoon teas. The wires were everywhere covered in ivy, the bars were twined in eglantine, honey-suckle and in thick trembling vines that lined the roofs of

37

the cages. I walked through the empty zoo and heard a few parakeets squawk, I saw the flash of a pink flamingo rising from a pool, I saw a treetop swarming with small green monkeys, but all the great animals seemed vanished. I felt a sudden wash of disappointment and realised then that I had come here to find my beast's prototype. He was no cousin of those chattering monkeys or those squawking birds. I came to a pool then and saw a ripple break the covering of thick green slime. A seal's shape curled out of it, its back speckled, even coated in this weight of green. His glistening, troubled eyes made me feel more akin to him. Then he dived and left the surface unbroken once more.

I was walking through a tunnel of vines when I heard footsteps. I bent beneath the hanging branches, as fearful as before. The gardens were free now, to animals as to humans, and yet my fear kept me cowed. There was the dusty odour of evergreen leaves. Then another scent crept through it, the scent of quite a different place. I ventured out to those approaching footsteps and recognised her walk.

She was carrying a black handbag, swinging on the crook of her arm. She did not seem to be aware of it. She was wearing a fawn hat which made a circle of shadow round her face. I swear I could smell the perfume from where I was. Her high heels clacked and clacked as she walked nearer, her eyes searched around constantly. She was on time, I gathered, as I must have been. When I stepped out in front of her path, she didn't show fear or surprise, only a familiar gladness.

I took her arm without any hesitation. We walked through the vines and out the other side, where once there was a reptiliary. The shed skins of its old inhabitants lay scattered about, colourless and wafer-thin. Her heels clattered off the tiled floor. She told me more about her life, but asked no questions at all about mine. Why I found this so comforting, I wasn't sure, but walking round the glass cases, my arm fell about her waist and hers around mine. We came to the exit sign and walked through, finding ourselves on a long green lawn. Even under the rolls of bandage and under her cotton dress, I could feel the bones of her hips and the movement of her skin above them. We sat down on the lawn.

Take it off, she said, pulling off my eyeshade.

Don't you mind, I asked, feeling drops of sweat fall down my outlandish forehead. She had a matter-of-fact air, however, that made such questions seem redundant.

You look tired, she said.

I was tired. She took my head between her hands and laid it on her lap. She stroked my forehead and my matted hair then, while talking in a deep, hypnotic voice about the project and herself. While she talked, although my back was to her, I could see the limpid shapes of her eyes before me. She talked of the complaints of everybody around her, of the hundreds of minor dissatisfactions they gave voice to daily. She herself, she told me, felt a dissatisfaction that was deep, but that she knew would never end, so what was the point in voicing it? She told me how heat appealed to her, she could wear light cotton dresses and always kept a colourful supply of wide-brimmed hats for going out in the sun. She told me how her life to others seemed to follow no shape, since she never worried or guarded against the diminishing future. But she said that the fact was that while she did accept most of what happened to her, she would have a premonition of important events some time before they occurred, as if to prepare her for them, so she could take advantage of them. She had felt that when she first heard the name musk.

I turned my head and looked up into her face. I put my hand on her knee as I did so. Take it off, she said, and began to unroll my bandages. I protested, but she whispered, in this persistent voice, that it could do no harm. She unwound it and unwound it till the first hairs began to appear between the white, and then the huge fist was exposed. She put my hand on her knee then and wrapped my elongated fingers round it. I felt her whole knee in the cup of my hand.

She told me more about herself. I could see long machines cutting corn in swathes as she talked. She talked of herself as if she were describing an acquaintance she had known for years, but never well enough. There was a girl, I gathered, before the woman. The thought that we all had some past was becoming difficult for me. But looking at her I could see her face diminish into the other she must have been. She stretched out her leg so that her knee straightened under my fist. Some bright green-coloured birds flew out of the cedars. I felt her knee change shape once more as she bent her long leg at an angle under my chin and began to talk about the beauty. My voice sounded deeper than ever and so I turned my head to see if it had alarmed her. What I found was her eyes staring wide at me in a way that left no doubt that each was understood. I told her about the sounds I had discovered beneath the surface of things, the hum from the girders, the mauve twilight. As the surface of everything becomes more loathsome, I said, thinking of the thing I was, the beauty seems to come from nowhere, a thing in itself.

40

She leaned towards me and again I knew I had been understood. But the pleasure of that thought brought an anxiety with it, as to whether she had been. She took my face in her hands, she was smiling. How long was it, I wondered, since I had felt uncalloused skin against my own? The beauty came in a rush. Joy was the word I thought of, joy I knew then was that word for when beauty was not only seen or heard, but felt from inside. The sound of it was all around me. Her eyes were the brown of burnt heather, with tiny flecks of gold in the dark. They glowed as she bent her head down towards me and rested her lips on mine.

The green birds must have flapped closer, because I heard their cries, one after the other so that they became a throaty purr. How I admired her boldness, in meeting my lips which must have changed beyond recognition. The rest of me must have learnt a new suppleness, however, for while still lying on her lap I managed to turn and raise her above me in the same embrace. Can I describe the garment that wrapped round the top of her legs? She murmured again and smiled, and again I thought of her descriptions of herself as not herself. She gave a small cry as of a bird released and all the green parrots flew into the air at once. Her limbs wrapped round me, each one seemed interchangeable, always with the same texture, and I knew then that I had a soul for she met it, embraced it and breathed on it with her own. We lay there, brute and beauty, a small curtain of pollen seeming to fall on us as if cast off from the blue skein above. There was a dry flowered smell.

It was some time before we rose. My soul had twisted itself into a knot that it would keep, for ever, I thought. We walked back through the arboured tunnel. Her heels

41

clicked once more against the path. She told me that the insides of her legs were wet. She rested her hand on the crook of my arm. Behind us tiny animals followed, unseen, only present by the noises they made, small whisperings and rustlings as if to celebrate the hour that had passed. We agreed to revisit the reptile parlour, then to go for the time being on our separate ways.

Even as we walked through the shattered awning, I was made aware of further changes, by the minute. The skins of dead reptiles hung off the vines and as we walked beneath we set them swinging, collapsing the remaining panes into shivers of crystal. How wise of that genus, I remarked to her, to cast off a surface with each new season. She rubbed her nail up and down my forearm and told me more about her childhood.

I listened as she talked about books, how an unlettered farm girl would remove them from a large tea chest beneath her father's workbench and phrase to herself the long words, few of which she understood. They seemed a secret knowledge to her, and when she came to work in galleries, her surprise at the fact that others shared it was only matched by their surprise at the freshness her childhood knowledge had retained. Several times I tried to answer but found my voice retreating once more to the deep cavern of my throat. As the words went, then panic came that the essence of that hour we had spent was vanishing, shedding itself in turn. She turned to me suddenly, as if noticing this, on instinct. It is time to go, she said.

Before leaving she wrapped me carefully once more. We left by different entrances. I walked back down the long avenue and knew that each change that happened was reflected in that bowl-like essence that lay somewhere beneath the skin. The avenue was empty of people, the shadows slept at the feet of the trees, long and somehow full of ease. My feet moved over the grass, faster and then faster, I felt abandoned beneath those trees and dared to move out into the open fields. I saw a mark on my wrist and made out a number, in stately blue ink, barely smudged. She had written it there. Everything would be for the best I felt, having no knowledge of what awaited me.

10

᙭᙭᙭᙭᙭᙭

Travelling in the mauve light at the irregular time that I did, the train was quite empty. The city barely rippled in that light, the soldiers had left it, the water lay still to my right like a sheet of well-tempered glass. My vision was obscured with a fringe of hairs to the left and right of the oval it had become. I sensed this was caused by the growth round my temples. But it leant a charm to that seascape, fringed by rainbows that threw into relief that gunmetal blue. Then all the light bled from the carriage, my shadow came to match the tint of the metal floor. I felt suddenly darker. The train lurched on its sweep forwards, as if dragging me towards some armageddon.

And small gusts of spray blew over me when I came to the gardens. There was wind at last. I thought of the conversations that wind would make around evening tables. There was a slow dull pain in the palm of my hand. I looked down and saw that my fingers were curled like clams. I had mislaid my briefcase.

The front door was ajar. I made my way through the house. I could hear Matilde or Marianne or both moving round upstairs but I didn't call. I felt they had heard me. Something moved me through the house and out of the French windows on to the lawn. I stood by the sundial amid the mounds of cut grass. I felt Marianne's eyes

44

approach the window upstairs but didn't turn or look. I tried to imagine what she must see below her, but no effort on my part could make that leap. Sure of what I felt like, all images of what I looked like were beyond me. Was I rotund, I wondered, did these luxuriant clumps of hair spill out from the crevices of what served as my garments, intimating the chaos inside? Or was the hair in fact quite sparse, did the flakes that I left behind me like gossamer cover my cheeks, my fingers, every centimetre of available flesh that wasn't hidden by cloth? I remembered that my skin at times had made her uncomfortable. Did she remember that now, I wondered, and then realised how futile it was. All I could gauge was that whatever creature was filling her gaze had his left hand placed upon the disc of the sundial, the two largest fingers supporting the weight of his leaning body. I didn't dare return it. All I could bear was to call her name, my eyes fixed on the digits of the sundial, and wait for a reply.

I must have waited a long time for her voice, because when I became aware of my surroundings once more I was encircled by a halo of tiny insects. They hovered over the dial's copper surface, then up along my forearm, into a lulling, shifting crown around my head. The light that came through their penumbra was green, that strange pea-green aura I remembered from the first days of spring. Their combined hum was like the murmuring of angels. Their eyes were bright and green, and to my huge blue the magnificent swathes of their wings reduced to just that transparent glimmer. I remembered a glen, and her red hair surrounded by them, her long fingers flicking them from her face. I took my fingers from the sundial and began to walk back towards the house. They followed me, like a retinue all of my own,

45

but then they thinned as they approached the French windows, as if their proper home was outside. I entered the house with some sense of loss.

There was no meal in the kitchen. Once more I waited. I stood by the range feeling that to impose myself any further might be a mistake. I sensed a presence and heard a footfall behind the door, but could only see the door's gentle swing and the ghost of a shadow on the floor.

Have I become repugnant to you, I wanted to ask, as gently as the tilt of that door. But I feared the sound of my voice. So I waited to see would she enter, of her own accord.

The shadow departed and the footsteps retreated up the stairs. I kept my silence for a moment, and then thought of Matilde. The longing to say goodnight made me move once more. I crossed tile after tile of the kitchen floor. The scalloped shape of the soles of my shoes no longer suited my posture. I would have thrown them off and walked barefoot, but felt that would have worsened things. I pushed open the kitchen door and felt the resistance of tiles change to the softness of carpet. As I reached the bannisters there was a rustling above. I heard her voice.

Don't come up, she pleaded, Matilde's not asleep.

Please, my darling, I said, but the words sounded like heavy drops of oil, don't be afraid. I want to kiss her goodnight. I would have said more but I could feel her fear rush down the stairs towards me like a wall of water. I could by no means blame her, but that fear served to goad me even more.

Matilde, I called, hoping I could pronounce at least that. Marianne's sob answered me from above.

Come up then.

The top of the stairs was bathed in light. Marianne was there, a spiked baking tin in her fist.

Say goodnight from the doorway, she said.

Your voice, I tried to say, sounds as foreign as mine must be. Again the words curled beyond speech. I walked up slowly. She kept her metallic shield thrust towards me. I placed my palm against the spikes. The landing seemed unnaturally narrow. I followed her covered hand to a door.

Goodnight Matilde. I attempted the syllables slowly. The broad *a* reminded me of a field of grass and the *ilde* made me think of a thin bird flying directly upwards. I tried to picture both of these as I phrased her name, the thin bird flying directly upwards out of the sea of grass. To raise the timbre of my voice I contracted all of my throat muscles.

I heard no reply. I drew as quiet and deep a breath as I could and began again. Before I reached the first consonant, however, I felt a blow from behind. The metallic spikes scraped me like a claw, I fell headlong, I heard a door slam and a key turn in a lock with a short reverberant click.

11

The house fell into its evening mood, that mood of which one might remark how quiet it is. On the contrary, it was a harvest of sounds. I lay with my cheek on the carpet and listened. I knew now that I was not in Matilde's bedroom but in my own, or, to use the terminology of the past, our own. My fingers touched off a gossamer substance which seemed for a moment or so to be castaways of mine but which I discovered, as I pulled it towards my lips, to be a long silk stocking. I drew it through my lips and the smell of her skin came to me with a strength that it never had had before. I recognised the odour of the drops she added to her bath. Woman and the world that word implied seemed as strange a bestiary to me as the world I had become. I listened to the sounds and tasted the memories that smell brought to me. The moon was swelling into the rectangle of the window. I was in a bar with oak and gold-coloured fittings, waiting for her entrance. There was a door adjoining which led to a dancehall, and dancers surrounded me, some awaiting their partners, others already joined. I stood a little on my own, as if to express the pride I felt, knowing that when I held her in my arms I would want no other. I glimpsed myself in the bar-room mirror, quiet, saturnine, but above all, proud. They surrounded me in

48

couples but none would be as beautiful as she. Then she came in, wearing what she called her disgraceful dress. It was white, glittering with spangles, slashed all over with half-moons that showed her flesh. The dark silk of this stocking glowed beneath it, flashed black as she moved towards me and one leg parted her dress's sheath. We kissed at the bar, before the mirror, and moved towards the dancehall; even before we had approached it our movements blended into dance. We wove through those thousand couples and that perfume was our own.

The memory of that perfume was easier than her name. One by one the lawn sprinklers stopped their hissing. The insects that had thrived on the long heat beat against the window-pane, lit by the globule of blue light that the moon had become. The perfume waned and ebbed in my senses through the chorus that I once thought of as silence. My arms were tough as beetle-hide beneath me on the carpet. My lids were heavy but took a long time to close. Slowly, though, that chorus changed from bluish to black and I fell asleep.

12

≈≈≈≈≈

There were curtains of dark like curtains of silk, the blackest furthest away. There was one lone hair on an expanse of tan, which swathed off from me like a desert. At its base the earth swelled a little like a pore, then sucked inwards. And as I stood there it grew. Grew so much that it bent away near its tip, under pressure from its own weight. A tiny drop formed there, fell away and splashed at my feet. I began to walk over that undulating surface, through the curtains of dark. What had seemed darkest from some way off melted, as I approached, into the hue of what I had left behind. There were no humans in this landscape, though all about me was the aura of humanity. The darkness dispersed as I walked towards it, then formed again in the middle distance. I felt I would meet a woman here. Another smooth basilisk grew some way off, soaring from its pore beyond my field of vision. Around it grew neighbours, too smooth to be a forest, too separate to be a field. A drop splashed beside me, so large that it wet my ankles. Then another fell and another, so much so that the water rose to my waist, surged in a current and drew me away. Its colour I would have registered as blue, had the light been clear enough. I hardly swam, I was borne with it over that landscape that sank under its even progression. There were threads of hair beneath me, stroking my body like moss or water weed would, but of a more silken texture, long, flowing with the water, as if each strand was endless. I dared to put my feet down and felt the fleshly surface. I walked to a bank and raised myself up. The water ran below me now, the hair wafted with the flow. There was a woman some yards beyond me, on the bank. Two great webbed feet caressed the woman, her hair made fury with the water. All above me was the beating of wings. A white neck curled from the sky as if on a sudden impulse, its predatory beak turned this way and that. Was it the sight of me, I wondered, that made the sound of wings more furious, that caused those feet to rise, that white neck to coil about that woman, bearing her upwards? Her hair dragged itself from the yards of water and soared, whipping my face with droplets before it was gone. The bank from which she'd risen flooded with water, forming a pool. I made my way to it and bent. I saw my monstrous head reflected there, ringed by a circle of eggs. Were they the swan's, or the woman's, I wondered and lifted one of them out. The heat of my unruly paw was anathema to it, for the droplets of water began to sizzle and steam and a crack sped across the white surface. The sheaves of egg fell away and a cherub stood there, creaking its downy wings. One by one the other eggs split and the cherubs beat their way to the ceiling. They settled into niches in the plasterwork. There was the sound of falling water.

51

13

☒☒☒☒☒☒

When light finally spread over the contours around me and the clusters of colour gathered at each eyelid I found I was on the floor no longer. The bed was beneath me and the sheet was crammed into a ball, shredded in parts where my fingers had clutched it too ardently. There was a sound in the air which I could not immediately divine. I got to my feet and it was all around me, a steady thudding like the feet of many children. I went to the window where the light was. My eyes were unsteady as yet but when I pulled back the gauze curtain and gazed out on the unfamiliar, I saw it all. It was raining.

The water came in straight threads, the darkest ones furthest from my gaze. Had I dreamed that liquid, I wondered, from the constant sky. But I saw that in the gardens all about me the sprinklers had stopped, and gathered that others must hear it too. There was moisture in the air, that scent of dryness had vanished. My bandages clung like a mask.

There was the sound of a table being laid downstairs. I was not at all hungry. I squatted, held my knees close to my chin and listened to the downpour. Each echo that came from downstairs was different now, muffled by the falling water. Towards evening I heard music and the sounds of guests. I rocked backwards and forwards by the window. There was a rhythm to the falling water to which I responded. A kind of sleep came.

I dreamt I was in the room downstairs. A metronome ticked from the piano, with the sound of dripping water. I played, keeping my fingers on the black notes. Marianne stood above me. Matilde danced, in her confirmation dress, the white frills spreading as she turned. The liquid beat spilled over the piano though and soon my hands began to sweat. My bound fingers stretched for the notes, so that Bach was slowed to their shape. I knew it was going badly. Can we not try it again, I asked Marianne, but the russet stain was creeping from the black notes to the white, making them indistinguishable. The liquid thud from the mahogany frame began to wilt then, to melt into a gurgle. Matilde turned bravely but the wafer-like stiffness of her confirmation dress became sodden in turn. It hampered her movements, it clung round her knees like whipped cream. She twirled and twirled, but could not defeat it. Her tears made matters worse and soon her Crimplene elegance was plain grey, clinging to her sides. The greyness oozed from the keys, the same as the colour that bound me, and soon music, room and all of us were buried in its path. I saw their hair, twined just above that matter, in the shape of a fleur de lys. It bound and unbound itself as if in final parting, then too went under.

14

❧❧❧❧❧

The rains merged day into night and night into day again. The dull throbbing and the whispering of rivulets outside and the distant cascades of trains enveloped me. A light fungus grew on the walls, a furred coating of gossamer. I would loll against this vegetable surface, my breath wreathing the room in billows of steam which dripped in tears from the ceiling. So my room wept at intervals and the carpet vanished beneath a film of grey. My lungs, like sodden sponges, inhaled their own moisture. At intervals a plate was pushed through the door. I ate, but hardly noticed the textures. Each dish grew a web of its own. I slept and woke and slept again, lulled by those watering noises. My limbs ceased to concern me. There was a kind of peace in this moisturous world and I wondered once how it was regarded by the world outside. Morgan's eyeshade would be dispensable, I gathered, since the hard sunlight was no more. The streets would have changed from a dusty tan to a shimmering grey. I dreamed that perhaps my condition might have lessened. Then the rains stopped and I knew that I could dream no more.

15

𝕩𝕩𝕩𝕩𝕩𝕩

There was a calm, willow-green evening light. All the drops had finished but their liquid echo lasted for some time. Old sounds gained precedence, old but fresh because so long unheard. There was the crackle of burning fat from below. A plate clattered. Then came the hissing of sprinklers, like barely-discernible strings.

I rose, very slowly. My limbs stretched at their coverings, having grown in the interval. I knew there would be no reversal. Certain tendons felt like wads of bunched steel. I walked to the doorway. It was locked as before but I gouged round the keyhole with my nail. The wood splintered easily, the door swung open. Now that crackle of fat sounded louder and the pall of singed flesh slowly filled the room. But stronger than that was the pall of memory. I heard the front door open, the sound of voices, of entering guests. The door closed again and the voices fell to a murmur, broken by the occasional soft ringing of glass. I stepped on to the carpet. I thought of my appearance, but looked in no mirror, as mindful of my own terror as I was of theirs. The landing, which had once been planes and angles, throbbed as I walked through it, the ceiling seemed to congeal beyond me into a closed mouth and yet raised itself as I came forwards, as if parting its lips to let me through. The stairs whorled below me in turn. I followed the glimmer at the end of them, through which the sounds seemed to emanate. My fingers gripped the rail and my new hands left palm marks on the cedar wood. There was the door then, tall, soft-cornered and ringed with light. I stopped, listening to the voices. I meant to enter, but knelt first on the carpet and put my eye to the keyhole of light. I saw the dim shapes of figures round a table. Then the handle turned, the door fell from me and I collapsed inside.

There were kitchen tiles by my cheek once more. I saw the foot of Marianne, the long black heel rising to her ankle, and her hand, clutching the doorknob and her face, far above me. Her voice was raised, but the words I could not distinguish. I understand your anger, I said, I have become an embarrassment to you, I can see that clearly. But from my prone position on the tiles those words didn't sound like words. My darling, I tried again, perhaps it's better that I leave. Through the curve of her shoe's instep I could see that table, the dinner-lamp hanging low and the Ambrose couple, male and female, staring towards me with curved, craned heads. Marianne's foot rose and fell again, nearer now to my eyes. I inched backwards away from it as I felt I should. It rose again and the heel sang off the tiles. I gathered myself on to all fours. Do you remember that evening we danced, I began, but that heel numbed me into silence. I craned my head round and stared up at her face, which seemed larger than a full evening moon after wet weather. Should I go, I mouthed and the eyes, though they didn't seem to hear me, seemed pregnant with the word Yes. I backed away and sidled round the doorway, still longing for a contradiction. But the heel clacked off the doorway and the doorway clacked shut. I heard the rustle, the regretful whisper of the key turning. I raised my weighty palm to that door and gouged some words on the cedar. Goodbye.

16

✿✿✿✿✿✿

The dark had brushed all the gardens outside. Each lawn swam with what the rain had left and the cuttings of grass lay like moss upon the surface. I walked. I was watched only by the moon, which shone silver above me, swollen, as though it could contain any number of dreams. When I reached the tracks a few restful stars had joined it. The sleepers had swollen into giant sponges and between the lines of track, glowing dully with the rust it had gathered, a steady stream of water ran. I found night so much more comforting than day, each shape seemed like a disguise, each shadow a mask. A reptile slid down towards me through the waters, passing under my legs to the sleepers behind me. The city, when I reached it, gleamed with the metal of new rain. I walked along the river, glistening at last, laced with ropes of fungus and the pads of lilies. The bridge barely curved above its growth. It seemed now hardly necessary, the river at points spawned a bridge of its own, vegetable and massy, beneath which it remembered its liquid state. There was the steady moan of travelling water and a film of moisture followed its curve to the bay, and beyond to dimness. My feet padded over the metal bridge and their muffled echo seemed to come from beyond. A fish leapt clear of the lilies, gripped a moth in its jaws and plunged downwards once more. I walked, with no knowledge of where I was heading. Somewhere, I felt there was a place for me. And the bridge led me, as it only could, to the empty street alongside. There was a cobblestone archway ahead. A tangle of foliage hung from above. Through the olive-green leaves I saw an edifice glowing. I brushed the leaves apart with my arms and walked on towards it.

17

As with creatures whose bone structures enclose their flesh, ants, crabs and armadillos, lending support from without rather than within, so the girders of this structure bound the planes of concrete and glass. It was square-shaped, beetling over the tiny streets around. It threw more a mood than a shadow on its environs. Not a soul walked on the pavements around it and the mists, which were now dispersing elsewhere, seemed to cling to the brickwork for comfort. How had I not noticed it, I wondered, in what I was at last beginning to think of as my former life. I had the dim memory of waiting under that Dutch-style façade beyond for a cream-coloured bus. How long must that have been, I wondered, and how long did this immensity take to build and under what conditions of secrecy? It was a seat of some power, I sensed. The surface of the brick was smooth, even metallic, and it tingled gently under the pads of my fingers as if to give just a whisper of the power within. The mists rose to my waist, close to the wall. I walked along it, feeling that tremulous whisper. I reached a corner. It was sharp, seemed dropped like a plumb-line from the stars. I could then see large steps and a concrete patio leading to the miniature street. The dimensions of that street, once so snug and human, now seemed absurd.

This giant that scraped the stars had winnowed any purpose it might have once had. There were vast globes on the patio that lit it from the front. The building rose beyond their beam though, and vanished into gloom. The steps rose to plate-glass doors, higher than any human frame. They would have sufficed even for me.

I walked back beyond the corner to the girder-point. I removed the bandages from my palms and I began to climb.

Soon the mist was below me, and the patio, and the street. My cloths unwrapped as I rose. They made white flags in the breeze beneath me. Then even the clouds dispersed and the moon rolled yellow next to the clean line of brick. My shadow came with it, darkening the streets. The stars pricked the sky all over, the moon ladled over them and the wind whipped round my loosened limbs. It tore at my bandages, set them free then in one long roll from my waist. I had come to the end of the girder. There was a parapet above me. I paused, clinging with both hands to an overhang.

The last piece of white unravelled from my calf. I let loose one hand and grabbed the cloth with it, swinging freely. I was naked, I realised, but observed by nothing but the moon and stars; for one moment my body sang. I hung on, and each tendon felt at home. I looked up at the moon and whispered a sigh of thanks. The stars glowed brighter for a moment. I heard the wind and the furling of cloth. I let my eyes follow the bandage, which billowed in a long white arc, drawn into a curve by the high wind and tracing figures to the ground below me.

It was no longer empty. A small boy stood there. His hand was stretched in the air for the white end. It hung above him, moving back and forth. I considered what he would have seen and felt proud of myself, his eyes watching. He had the calm concentration of all children. I let the bandage go, as a message or gift, and swung myself in one movement over the parapet.

I thought of wheat fields at night, their yellow tips gleaming as the full sweep of the night sky came into my vision. All the stars had cleared themselves of mist for me, like hard bright cornheads waiting to be gathered. I balanced on that parapet without much difficulty. My toes gripped the edge while my heels still hung over the void. There was humming in the air. It had two pitches, bassy below and thin and wavering above. Did it come from those stars or this building, I wondered. I let my eyes fall with it from the wheatfields to what lay at my feet.

The roof was of plain cement with a spiral staircase jutting out into the skyline. Many yards away, near the opposite parapet, was a rain trough. I stepped down on to the roof and felt the cement beneath my feet.

The staircase was made of thin steel which sang when I plucked it. It made a dark half-segment through the roof. I climbed down, into the building below.

I found a long, low-roofed storeroom. There was a rolled carpet against the wall. Through the slim rectangular windows the wheaten stars could be seen. I crawled inside the cylinder of carpet and was soon asleep.

18

❧❧❧❧❧

My dreams were of humans. I was smooth once more, my hair was cut close to my temples, I was wearing a suit I had never seen, it is tighter in fashion than in my day I remember saying. Absolutely unfamiliar with myself, like one who has drifted off and been suddenly woken in mid-afternoon, I knew obscurely that what I carried under my elbow, pressed to my side, was a brief of some kind. I walked down a long corridor with flowers on the floor, there were sweeps of light coming through successive windows. When I came to the fourth door I knew that this was where my assignation was, though there was no indication that doors down the long corridor beyond were any different. I knocked, heard no answer but entered anyway.

She was standing by the window with some beads on the high-frocked dress which gave her figure the repose it had always promised. She was twisting the beads in her fingers. She did not look up when I entered, allowing me to see to the full what a woman she had become. The creature I had left, so small, so unformed, with those long ribbons of years ahead of her, had emerged, both bound and unwrapped by them, the child I barely knew so changed as to be almost hidden and quite another creature revealed.

Matilde.

She turned when I called her name. Like those exotic birds in whom, by reason of acquaintance with their more prosaic cousins, we recognise some characteristics, I could see in that long neck, in that tiny ruffle which seemed to spread from it to the crown of her short cropped hair, some ghost of her childhood movements.

She came towards me and kissed me. The kiss was a brief one, but in the quick withdrawal of her face from mine I sensed a torrent of emotion. I looked into her eyes and saw them at once angry and pleading for kindness. I knew then she was in love, she had been in love and felt mishandled. I felt pity, but even more, a sense of great misplacement that her body had touched another's, her soul had met another's. She called me by a name then, not my own, and it dawned on me that she was in love with me.

She asked me to reconsider my feelings. She told me no one but me could fill her life, now or for a long time to come; perhaps for ever. My coldness she could not understand, but she could live with it if I were to give even a hint of my former affection. Nobody could have been like me, she whispered, during those moments.

I wondered what I had done, how I had met her, how I had kept my identity secret. But the light that came through the great plate-glass window from what seemed to be a workaday, silver-lined city outside imposed its own order on my words, my movements. I felt the great ageful wash of guilt, I must have known, obscurely, in the pit of the consciousness with which I performed whatever acts I had performed, who and what I was. It inhibited my words even more. She was bathed in that

64

light, so proud and vulnerable, shifting backwards and forwards, her tall comely shape like a product of it, so statuesque and proud, waiting for words I could never utter now I knew who I once was, what I later was, to her. At last she took my silence with finality. She became as shapely, as functional as that light.

The light surrounding her was oblong and tall, suiting her proportions. Then the light changed and all the angles softened and I was staring now at a circular orb as rich as morning. There were rainbows in front of my eyes and the multitudinous curve of those hairs once more. Like sedge-grasses or rushes sweeping down a dune, they glistened with pinpoints of moisture as if Morning herself had bestowed them upon her, sucked through that invisible line between light and dark. I knew then it was my arm, on which my large head was resting. The long funnel of carpet was up there, a mouth of light. The morning sun filled it almost totally, distorted only by the grime on the plate-glass window. I stared at this sun for a long time. It as golden as ever, but no longer an orb. It was blessedly elliptical, as if the lenses of my new eyes had given it depth. Then the sun was eclipsed by a shape that entered its curve abruptly and hung there, wavering slightly, its edges blurred. Was it cherub or flying creature, I wondered, hovering just beyond the edges of that plate-glass; until it spoke then, and in a boy's voice.

I brought you your things, sir.

The voice was high-pitched and eager, with a slight hint of the Americas. I wondered what being would call such as me sir. I dragged myself towards the light. His face withdrew somewhat, then approached again. A hand stretched.

I kept these for you. The way you climbed that building was really something.

His hand was firm and surprisingly strong. It grasped mine until I clambered out. I rose to my full height and stretched myself. I could feel his eyes on me constantly, admiring and awestruck. I almost shared his wonder at my movements. The air was cut in half with the light which slanted in one rigid plane, darkened my upper half and lightened my lower. There was a plain white marble block by the window. I sat on it, my knees became half-orbs of grey. The marble was cool, chalk-smelling. I placed my chin in the palm of my hand and looked up from the repose of myself to his face.

I kept them for you, he repeated. They're as good as new.

He held the bandages in his tiny hands. The first stirrings of haze began in the city behind him. The bandages were amber-coloured; last night's rain had sullied all the white. He held them out as if presenting a gift. And when I took them from him I felt the mood of my last self rise like steam off them, they carried an odour like the juices of a thousand memories, if memories could have been crushed like grapes or rose petals. I let them drop to the floor and a cloud of dust rose from them, as if they were unwilling to say goodbye.

Is there anything you'd like? he asked.

I had been reluctant to speak, remembering the loathing that my voice once produced. But I trusted in his trust of me. I told him slowly and carefully that yes, I did feel hungry.

What do you eat?

And I realised for the first time that I was not sure. I had the memory of what had once been a tongue shredded on

66

a plate, and of murmuring voices. Had I not eaten since then? I told the boy I was not sure. He described, his eyes wide open and eager, the various kinds of foods that he could get me. His father grew sweetcorn in the basement, where the heat from the immense boiler that he stoked let them grow to 'that size' – and he stretched out his arms. There were leftovers from the office canteen. He could even get me whole dinners, at a pinch.

I imagined the broad green leaves of the sweetcorn and so asked him for that. He ran to the door then, but stopped there and turned. He stared at me. His brown eyes seemed almost embarrassed.

Is there something wrong? The timbre of my voice was by now like whole forests. His eyes flashed towards me and away.

I want to see you walk.

So I rose from the marble block and took his hand in mine and walked to the plate-glass window. Every tendon seemed to stretch like never before. The light filled me when I reached it. I let go of his hand and pressed both arms against the glass. The glass, which transmitted such heat, was itself like ice. My forearms blazed with colour. I turned to see was he happy, but he was gone.

I felt the light come through me. I walked up to the spiral staircase and climbed outside.

19

The city had grown its coating of haze, so thick that the skyline imitated a horizon, an even murky blue, but for the largest buildings which soared above it. Periodic gusts of hot winds spread across it, dragging me now in one direction, now in the other. I was drawn towards the cement pool and there saw myself again, with wonder now and a touch of delight. The water was miraculously still, maybe four feet deep. I was fawn in colour, strange elegant angles like curlicues whorled where my elbows were. Underneath the tawny sheen my limbs seemed translucent, changed into some strange alloy, gelatin perhaps, opaque where the bones might have been. I could have stretched for an age. I slid into the water then and assumed its element. Threads of gold flowed out from me, shifting with the ripples. I rolled my head under and around and came to the surface again, dreaming of that hair again that flowed towards a bank. Two great webbed feet were splayed above it. There was the sound of flapping wings, the sky was muddied by white and the feet slowly rose, underneath the bales of beating feathers. A large egg rocked there, backwards and forwards. A line streaked across its surface, then a regular crack which grew, emitted small bursts of chalk dust. The sides of egg split, two wings struggled to light and a

Phoenix head above them, a jabbing, mareotic beak turned this way and that. It grew to fullness then flew, again the flapping bales of feather drew the webbed feet upwards. The fragments of shell tumbled into the water and hissed there, bubbling gently. Something green floated among them. I gripped it between two fingers. It was a head of corn.

The boy stood by the pool's edge, his thin arms folded round a host of green corn-tips. He smiled and I saw for the first time a gap between his teeth. I slid from the water to the pool's edge. I ate the corn slowly and he ate one too, as if to share the moment with me. I peeled the broad green leaves which the wind whipped away over the parapet into the haze beyond. He told me how the corn struggles through its envelope of green and only throws it off when it attains perfect ripeness. Has that happened to you, he asked. I answered that I could not be sure.

He told me then how his brown complexion came from stoking the enormous stoves which powered the building which his father, the boilerman, kept under his charge. He had stoked them for six years, and was now aged twelve. He asked me my story and I told him of the changes, the bandaged dinner-parties and the escape into the night. He nodded, and seemed to understand. I remembered Marianne and Matilde, and standing by the sundial underneath the fencing, and my cheeks moistened with tears. I felt a pain where my heart should have been and my shoulders began to heave with uncontrollable sobs. He put his hands on my temples and laid my head on his minute shoulder. He told me of dreams he had of changes, that his father was in fact a king who lorded over quite a different building in a large suite, serviced by a glittering lift.

Will nothing bring you back? he asked.

I told him I was not sure. He spoke to me then of wizards, of magic potions and maiden kisses. He kissed me on the fingers, as if to see could that effect a cure, and his eyes took some time to change from hope to disappointment. Then he confided in me that his disappointment would perhaps have been greater if I had changed back since nothing could be as splendid as what I was now.

There was a rumble in the building then and the liquid in the pool broke into ripples. That sound started up, both high and low at the same time. They were the boilers, he told me, starting up for the day. He would be needed to run errands and stoke them. Was there anything else I needed?

And I remembered her then. Like a clear liquid that one drinks with very special meals, the taste brought back that perfume, that dark hat moving among the drawing boards, those long knees in the reptile house. We had both shared the changes. My longing to see her was as sharp for a moment, as brutal, as all that had happened. I held my pliant wrist, remembering the bandage she had written on. I told him there was a number, written on the bandages down by the carpet-roll, could he ring it and tell her I was here.

I saw him run across the large empty slabs below, the white bandage streaming after him. He stopped at the edge of the street to roll it in a ball, but it unwound when he ran on again, trailing through the morning crowds. I sat on the parapet, feeling somewhere that I should think of things, but my thoughts resisted any shape. Each minute brought a mood of its own to which I succumbed.

So morning passed in a series of changes. Every moment presented a different vista. The winds blew in one and died down in the next. The sun kept its heat but moved perceptibly, bringing all its shadows with it. All the creatures of the air seemed to cling to the shadows and move with them too. Towards noon they settled as if the heat had lulled them at last and they knew that the shadows, decreasing since daybreak, could only grow. The pool steamed gently. I began to walk. I paced around my rectangular home and the creatures rose in flurries with each step. They seemed to anticipate each of my movements and cleared the warm concrete under my feet before each of my footfalls. I paced the concrete for what seemed an age. Each brick was infested with life. More creatures whispered from the crevices in the parapet. I stared over the edge at that great sweep of concrete and glass, and that whisper became a roar.

There was the sound of footsteps and I turned as she emerged from the spiral staircase. The wind came from below now and tugged at her dress and the straw basket she was carrying. The boy came out behind her. He stood watching as she walked towards me past the pool. I stood with my back to the parapet. She had a flowered dress. A stick of bread jutted from the basket. I went to move but none of my muscles would answer. The wind lifted her dress in gusts like the bowl of a hyacinth over the stems of black stocking which covered her knees. I felt strangely transparent under her gaze, as if she could see as she approached every cranny of me, down to that strange heart of mine still woven into a bowl from that afternoon of animals.

My darling –

She held out her hand and touched mine. Slowly the

71

whole of me rose to attention. The boy stared from behind her. Her only expression was a smile.

You are different again.

She drew me down beside her to tell me about the world. The company Musk had gone bankrupt, the product vanished without trace. And Morgan? I asked. She had called three days in succession, she told me, found the office closed and then transformed into a manicure salon. Do things change so fast out there? I asked. Everything, she answered.

I thought of Morgan and how our years together would vanish without trace. The wind lifted her hair and transformed it utterly.

Can I embrace you? I asked her.

When she smiled in reply I put my arms around her, felt how they stretched with ease down below her spine to the tops of her thighs. She stroked my back, which seemed to mould itself into her hand's movement. I could picture the shape it assumed, a scallop, ridged to its base by her five long fingers. She drew one finger from the hollow of my temple down the long plane of my cheek and buried it in the golden strands of my torso. I lifted her in both hands, one beneath the small of her back and the other behind her knees, and walked with her to the parapet. She laid her cheek on the concrete and her eyes followed each one of my movements. Behind the flame of her hair the city steamed in its haze. My largeness was apt at last, my three fingers stretched the fabric of her dress, they exuded a warmth that filled her eyes, I was nothing that I had ever known or imagined. I carried her to the pool and dipped her slowly just beneath its surface. The green corn leaves floated everywhere, clinging to her body as I lay with one arm stretched on the bank, the other rippling the water. She made a crown of thick dark olive with the leaves. And as she played with me I changed, the hair of my forearm became sleek and shining, my fingers bunched like the feet of cattle. She nudged against my ear and drew one arm around me, wrapping the long strands of my tail about her neck. The boy made a wide fan of the corn-leaves and beat the air repeatedly to cool her. We played all afternoon under the boy's slow, quiet eyes. They filled with our delight and delighted us in turn. I saw a band of gold glistening in the water. I brought it to the surface and saw it was a wedding-ring. Long, slow tears coursed down my face then. She brushed them clear with her hands, but they kept on coming. And as if they understood my need, they held me while I wept, filling the pool to its brim, tears spilling over the sides. By evening, the whole parapet was wet.

She left with the last of the light. It held on barely, very barely, while she travelled down the core of the building. I saw her make that short, hesitant run across the piazza below and on to the empty street. The darkness slowly filled the air behind her, as if only my gaze had been willing it back. The way the inky blue of Matilde's palette gradually merged with and swamped the pink, that way the night invaded each yard of street as she passed over it.

20

The moon then came up and spread its own brand of light, and its image in the water was rippled by the wind. I was content to lie and measure its ascent and observe the gradual appearance of the stars. The spiral staircase became etched with silver. In my naivety, my joy, I had neglected to ask either of them about what lay below. That anonymous hum which even now persisted seemed to imply any number of worlds. I made my way to the staircase, swung myself on to the whorl of metal and crept downwards. I saw the concrete room and remembered my bedding in that roll of carpet. Below that again I found a hall of wires. They spread in all directions, all shapes and colours, from the tiniest to cables the circumference of my torso. The humming, so anonymous above, had grown a certain depth down here, as if each wire carried its own note, from the thinnest soprano to the basso-profundo of the thick-set cables. I thought of the music of insects, so ravishingly conveyed to me that garden afternoon. Each sound then had seemed bred of chance; no graph, no logical architecture, could have determined the glorious chaos of that chorus. But here, purpose seemed to reign. The wires sang in unison, with a constancy that had an end in view, an end I could only guess at.

The end must have been in that building, or perhaps the building itself was an end. With this in mind I made my way across the hall of wires to what had the appearance of a lift-shaft. The array of white buttons was discoloured with age. Too small for the pads of my fingers; I had to press them at random several all at once. I saw hawsers glisten through the metal grid, I heard the clicking of grease and the whir of a motor. And then the trellised box of the lift rose towards me.

We sank downwards through the building, the lift and I. Those dim halls rose to my vision and away again, each much like the one before. The buttons I had pressed must have determined our passage, because we stopped, unaccountably, in a felt-lined corridor without much distinction. I stepped through the trellised doors. I was half-mindful of going forward, half-mindful of going back again, when the doors slid closed. The lift whined and the light on the panel sank downwards.

I walked forwards. There were doors off this corridor, with rooms leading to more doors. What I had assumed to be devoid of life I soon found to be a bestiary. A deep-piled room seethed with mice. A moth watched me from a filing-cabinet. His eyes, full of the wisdom of ages and the fierceness of his few hours here, seemed to require my attention. My ears swelled with a sensation I could hardly feel as sound, let alone speech, and yet I felt from his quivering wings the urge to converse. I brushed him on to my palm. His glance seemed to harden – with disdain, it seemed – and his wings beat their way skew-wise towards the doorway.

I followed. His uneven flight, irritating but somehow alluring, drew me down stairways, passages, lit only by the fierceness of his glare. We were now in low-roofed concrete tunnels, similar in texture to the ones I had left, far above. He blundered into walls and cables, but somehow always kept ahead of me. Then that jagged flutter changed to a spiral of panic. I heard an unearthly trill, like the vibration of a toughened tongue in a mouth of bright leather. I turned and saw the scythe-like wings of a bat swoop by me, then change its flight into those jagged arpeggios the moth was now weaving. They traced each other in counterpoint for a moment and it seemed a second cry rang out with the bat's, a cry that was soft, like the sound pollen would make brushing off a wing, but yet a cry with more pain in it than any I had heard. Their paths merged into one then, the bat's mouth opened, then closed, and the bat flew on alone.

The corridor seemed like a tomb to me afterwards. That ashy cry seemed to echo down it, bringing tears to my eyes which made the walls glow. I made my way to the corridor's end, hoping for a lift or concrete stairs. The tunnelled walls curved and were lit by a glow that seemed brighter than the rainbows of my tears. It was yellowish, it flickered, there was a rhythmic, scraping sound. I heard voices then, one old and masterful, the other young. I came to the corner and saw the boy in the distance shovelling coal into a furnace. The heap he shovelled from was replenished from a source unseen. His shovelling was too tender to keep his heap down to size; it kept growing until it almost engulfed him. He was goaded on by shouts, coarse and violent. Then a dark-skinned figure in dungarees appeared, shovelled furiously with him for a moment, sent him spinning towards the furnace with a blow and left again, admonishing him to work faster.

21

When the boy appeared the next morning with his arms full of cornheads and that glad expression on his face, I didn't mention what I had seen. I breakfasted on the corn and watched the leaves whirl over the city on the early-morning wind. Even that wind seemed to partake of the savagery of last night's events. The mists slowly disappeared, revealing the tiny beads of the morning crowds. I bathed in the pool and as he washed each sinew, I noticed weals on his body where before I had been aware only of that dusky tan. I questioned him on the rules of the building, though. He told me that he worked by night, and by day the building fed upon the heat he had generated. The corridors were peopled by secretarial ranks and the whirr of office machines took over from the more ancient machines of the night. I asked him was he tired by day and he told me that he was, but the pleasure of my presence kept him awake. I told him that once my presence brought very little pleasure, to man or to beast, and he answered that he could not imagine how this could have been so. After a time he slept in my waterlogged arms. I wrapped myself round him, to accommodate his dreams.

I awoke to find her standing above me. It must have been early afternoon. I whispered at her to be silent and placed him beneath the shade of the parapet. We became lovers once more, then many many times. The concrete bubbled with our perspirations and we took to the pool for refreshment. She floated there, staring into the sky as I told her of the bat and the helpless moth. She told me that life had its own laws, different for each species. Does one law not rule us all? I asked her. How can it, she answered, or else we would have seen it. I asked her was there a law for me, as distinct as those for the bat and the moth. If there were, she asked me, would you obey it?

I had ceased to think of thoughts as thoughts, for the effort to separate them from the clouds of sensation that germinated them was mostly beyond me. Now, however, I pulled at this thought, I needed it clear, abstract and separate so as to find an answer. Her head played around my armpit then gradually fell asleep. I remembered dimly a tale of a beast who cried to the world to reveal him his destiny, to send him a mate. If there was a law for the bat, for the moth, for the woman, there must be a law for me, a law as succinct and precise as those laws I obeyed when walking past the whispering gardens each day to work. But how to find out this law, and the destiny it implied? But then, it occurred to me, walking by those gardens, along the torrid tracks, I had been no more aware of what law I obeyed than I was now, obeying no law at all. If asked then, was there a pattern, a plan, I would have said no, categorically no. So law, if law there was, revealed itself in retrospect, like a sad bride coming to her wedding too late to partake in it.

My efforts at thought exhausted me and these fancies gradually sank into that well of sensation from which they had emerged. The darkness seeped around me, like a torpor brought on by my mood. It was indeed night. She still slept in the niche of my arm. I lifted her head and placed it at my navel, and curled around each of her limbs to make her sleeping easier. The wind ruffled her tangled clothing and set the down along her cheekbones alight. I thought about what laws bound us and she opened her eyes then, as if in answer to that thought. Her lids parted slowly to reveal my curved reflection in her pupils. I stared at myself for a time, for perhaps too long a time, seeing me, seeing her, seeing me in her. Only when her eyes were fully open did I become aware of her expression. She took a sharp intake of breath. The horror filled her limpid eyes as the night had filled mine. She drew backwards. I raised my hands to clutch her, too roughly. Please, I whispered. It's the night, she said, you're different. No, I cried. She was standing now, walking backwards towards the staircase. You should never have let me sleep, she whispered. The dark moulded her like a curtain, her hair glowed like sullen rust. I can't help my fear, she whispered, you should never have let me sleep. Her hand searched for the metal staircase. No, I whispered again, but my whisper gathered like a roar. She ran from that wall of sound. Somewhere above me, stars began to fall.

22

I lay for a long time. The darkness weighed on me. Who would remember the extraordinary length of her legs, I wondered, who would delight in that softness of skin at the joint of her knee, if not me? The changes came with such rapidity. Was the air never to be still, I wondered, from one moment to the next? To whom could she tell those stories, of the large tractors swathing through the meadows, of the young girl walking through the dew-soaked stubble? And even now the pace of my grief was such that I could feel it entwining me in a skin of its own. She had seen something, I remembered, something that caused the fear, and I rose slowly to my feet and staggered to the water. All I saw there was a shadow, like some more essential shade of dark than that which surrounded me. And I managed the thought that even what she had seen was now part of the past. Yet the desire to see what she had seen persisted. I made for the building below, searching out a mirror.

The lift was made of trellised bars of metal. None of its surfaces conveyed the ghost of a reflection. I pressed the buttons for some level below. I heard the whine of the motor, and with it a sound that was not a sound, that was above sound, that was a sensation, around my skull, my cheekbones, like the needle-points of a sandstorm. I raised my hands to my cheeks to locate it. Then this sound took shape, flowed into vowels and syllables, into sentences. It spoke.

You operate this lift, it said, like someone remembering what it was to travel in it. And yet you look like –

What do I look like? I asked. I closed my eyes. The voice began again.

You take your texture from whatever surface you inhabit. In this lift you belong to that odour of grease, hawsers and trellised metal. Outside it, I would have no idea.

I opened my eyes. I saw opposite me, clinging to the bars, a bat. His eyes were bright with reason. I remembered the arpeggios of fear and the death of the moth. That leatherish mouth didn't move, and yet his voice sang all around me.

Can you fly? he asked.

I shook my head.

Each animal function, he told me, has its sister emotion. Loathing, he said, has been your companion for some time.

He moved his head and seemed to smile. Do you wish to fly?

I nodded.

Take us up, then.

I pressed the buttons. He stared as we swayed upwards once more, a stare full of brightness, whimsy, intelligence.

23

He clung to the matted hair on my arm as I walked from the staircase. I placed him on the parapet. His sightless eyes turned in their sockets. I could feel his voice again, prodding me like gorse. Forget wings, he told me. Watch!

He moved both arms as if stroking the air, stepped off the parapet and plummeted like a dead weight. I cried out in alarm, but saw his fall, of a sudden, transform into a graceful curve. It became a figure of eight and slowly drew him upwards once more. He hovered above me for a moment, full of cries.

Wings are quite useless, he said, mere symbols of our activity. Birds, being vainer than my species, love to proclaim their importance, cover themselves in feathers and tails they can fan. But all one needs to fly with is desire.

And I thought of how swallows always reveal themselves in spring like small threads of longing and as the heat grows they become rushes of memory, filling the air with their curlicues, never touching ground, symbols indeed of desire.

Do you desire? he asked me.

I had hardly thought before I flew. The parapet swung above me and the piazza grew larger, swum before my eyes till I left it behind and moved in a long curve down Dame Street, barely at the level of the second windows, piercing the rim of that layer of heat that the night hadn't yet dispersed. I took the breeze on my left side at Nassau Street and swept down that channel of air. Some instinct drew me towards the river. I felt his voice all around me again and glanced up to see him at my shoulder, his wings dipping easily and gracefully with my infant movements.

Lead the way, he whispered, so I swung him down the steaming river and then left, face above the railway tracks, under the long glass awning, through those arcs of spray that splashed on the night trains. We kept close to the rails as sleeper after sleeper sped below us, each like a resinous wall. I smelt the odour of cut grass then and rose and skimmed above garden after garden till at length I came to one where the blades had not been cut and recognised it as mine. I headed over the tips of the nodding grasses, barely able to see through the pollen. There was an immense triangle jutting from a metal plinth. I hovered over the heiroglyphs on the disc below and saw how the moon's cast upon time was at variance with the sun's. I saw a large ball of light somewhere up ahead. I left the sundial and made my way through the grasses once more. The ball of light beckoned through the clouds of pollen and then the air suddenly froze. I beat myself against it, but to no avail, the light was there, but sealed behind it, impenetrable. I had almost exhausted myself when I recognised the frozen air to be glass, the ball of light a flickering bulb. I slid downwards. A large jewelled palm wiped moisture off the pane. Through the swathe that was cut in it I could see a glass, half-filled with liquid and the same hand lifting it to the crescent space between lips. I was indeed home. I watched Marianne for what seemed an age, from below. In my absence her lips had changed from deep cherry to rust, her hair had been shorn tight, the corners of her eyes had grown two black triangles. Two fingers indented themselves on her cheek and the dome of another's head descended for another's lips to meet hers. I recognised James.

There was a letting-go and a sensation of ice sliding past my cheek. I fell down among the grasses below. Her lips, though larger to me than ever, were still those lips I remembered. Down among those roots of green I could still picture the kiss, too long, far too long for the desire that had carried me here. I tried to beat myself upwards but not a whisper of movement ensued.

I felt the air stroking my face then in soft hushes, and his voice sang round me once more.

You know now why bats are what they are, poised between strutting and flight. To fly cleanly you must learn pure desire, a desire that has no object. Any attachment to things of the world leaves you earthbound once more.

I held a pure blade of grass between my palms and imagined pure desire. I could picture nothing, and soon nothing was all I pictured. Slowly, very slowly, the memories left me. The house, the hissing sprinklers, the sundial. That window was the last memory to go, and the kiss drifted away like whorling water, and I rose, to hover inches over the lawn. He chirped with a pleasure that made me soar. Soon the house became a tiny dot in the palette of the blue earth below us.

24

The city sank, like a glass bead into a muddied pool. The air was pure above it, with the ethereal blue of a wedding-gown. He seemed not to move, but yet was all movement, rising above me. Desire, he said, when purified, becomes desire no longer. I felt his voice and soared with the certainty. Loathing, when purified, becomes loathing no longer. I felt all affirmation and drifted towards him, his eyes glowing sightless in the gloom. Through blindness, his voice sang out, we cultivate the vision, through sensation we reach it and yet what we reach we still cannot see. He drifted around me like a thread of silk. Yet the feeling, he whispered, is our only road there, so can we doubt that the feeling is all?

He drew his limbs about him and let himself fall. I fell to his pace, just above him. The air thickened and the streets billowed out below. There is a city, he whispered, to whose shape all cities aspire. And when the sheaves of our city fall away, we shall reach it. When will that be? I asked him. Tomorrow, he sang. He curled his furred body and sped downwards.

25

I stood alone on the parapet under the moon. Alarth – for that was his name – had vanished into the depths of the lift-shaft. The streets were empty and silver, like a dream that was now dreaming itself. I slid down from the parapet and walked towards the trough. I saw my face there, as limpid and clear as the moon beside it. Each breath I took was like a sliver of lost time. I inhaled and seemed to drink in hours. To each beginning there was an end, I knew, and each change hurried it nearer. I walked down the staircase to the comfort of the lift. I pressed the buttons and felt the gradual slide downwards. The cables of the lift swung, shifting their curves as they did so. I thought of the gardens, through the long heat and the rain, of Marianne's face with its triangles of black. That change, so miniature, had brought an ache to me as large as that the chaos of myself had brought to her. There was a law, I now knew, and its resolution would come to be. I pressed the buttons with the stumps of my arms. The door slid back and a corridor faced me, like all the others. There was no moonlight here to illuminate my way, but the discs of my eyes soon accepted the black and the dark became light of its own. A swarm of midges hovered round a door. I entered, and saw a room in the chaos that work had left behind. There were paper cups, the rinds of cheeses and a bottle of mineral water. There were drawing-boards ranged against the walls and across the slope of one of them a figure lay sleeping. I recognised the crescent of the green eyeshade and moved myself closer. Beneath the dull green shadow I saw Morgan's face, his lips immobile, a day or two's growth on his chin. He had vanished when she called, she had told me, and must have found different employment. I saw drawings crumpled beneath his head, those buildings of concrete and glass that had come to litter the city, half-finished. Conceived by nobody, it was generally imagined, and built in the owlish hours. Yet their source was here, in these immeasurable rooms. Spanning the wall behind was a miniature of the city as it once had been. I looked at those squares in their measured movement towards the river, their proportions so human, yet so perfect to the eye. I saw the park, etched out in strokes of green, the zoological gardens at its centre. I remembered the textures of pavements under my feet, of grass round my ankles, the doorways that once stared at my child's eyes, the balanced stone of their arches and the fanlights of glass. I saw drops splashing on Morgan's clenched hand and drew my lips down to taste the salt of my tears. The hand shifted then, the fingers stretched and touched my movable skin.

It is you, he said, after a moment's pause.

I nodded. His reddened eyes flashed under their arc of green.

What is it like, he asked, to be away from it all?

I shook my head. If I could have spoken I would have asked him not to talk, reminded him of our days without words in adjacent rooms. He rubbed his eyes and gestured round the room.

87

Each afternoon, he said, I draw the city for them. And each morning my instructions change.

Who are they, I would have asked.

I work for them now, he added. He gripped a paper cup and began rubbing it to shreds.

Do you remember the time, he asked, when we used to work until five and walk down the river to our separate trains?

Yes, I said. The word came out round and true.

I sleep here now, he told me. I wake and I work and I sleep again. I keep the shutters down so that the light is the same.

I asked him would he mind if I pulled them back. He shook his head slowly and watched me as I did so.

A horse walked down the street below, moved sideways to avoid a bollard. A large poppy filled the window of a haberdashery.

I stretched out one arm and touched his green eyeshade. My palm, like a mucous membrane, let his face glow through it.

Is it fair, he asked me, to have given us the memory of what was and the desire of what could be when we must suffer what is?

I heard the gravel of dust in his voice, I saw smudges of graphite on his fingers. I phrased his name slowly. Morgan.

He looked up. I felt the wind of his despair. I rose slowly till my thighs were level with his face. Goodbye now, he whispered. He stepped forwards with me and opened the window. I heard it close behind me as I sank through the gloom outside.

The horse was walking slowly, his dark grace etched against the sweep of College Green. I felt tired, I had lost even the memory of desire. I sank into the poppy in the haberdasher's window. I clung to the pistil and the petals billowed round me, settling gradually into a pillow of red.

26

✄✄✄✄✄

I awoke to the sounds of people. My arms were curled
round that thrust of pistil with the dewdrop at the tip.
The morning sun had stiffened the petals, the red pollen
covered me as if their lips had bunched into a kiss. The
early crowds passed by, but as I stretched my limbs
groups of them gathered to stare. I drew myself
upwards, bending the pistil towards me. The dewdrop
fell on my face. They murmured as they watched, about
portents and signs. Two soldiers pushed to the front.
The pistil slipped from my hands then, I rolled down
the petal and came to rest at their feet.

A man in the livery of a hotel commissionaire called on
me to stand. One khaki leg prodded me, gently, but not
without authority. Whom do you belong to, a voice above
me asked.

I saw a small face thrusting through the thighs about
me, a pair of arms full of cornheads. I gestured, but was
unwilling to speak. Is he yours, the same voice asked,
when he made it to my side. The boy nodded, with
childlike pride and vigour. He pressed a cornhead into
my hands.

I ate, and listened. You must keep him inside, one of
the soldiers said, phrasing the words carefully, as one

does with a child. The boy nodded, took my hand and led me forwards.

The crowd parted in front of us, but followed from behind. The commissionaire protested from amongst them. The soldier reached forward and the boy began to run. I ran too, over the grass above the paving-stones, and as the crowd followed faster, I gathered him in my arms and lost them.

We wove our way through the desultory streets. We came to a hotel with a park beside it. There was a water-less fountain there. We climbed into its stone flower and feasted on the cornheads. Soon the petals were littered with green.

27

He told me he had searched for me through the depths of the building. He had waited for her, but she had never arrived. I told him I had flown, guided by a feeling that was nothing but itself. I had seen the city become a dot on the landscape and a blade of grass become a tower of green.

He told me then of Jack, who had planted a stalk that made a ladder to the skies, of how the story never told him what Jack found there. I would dearly love to fly, he said, turning his face to me. We will wait till evening, I told him, till that magic hour when our desires can picture the image that retreats from us. Will you fly to her? he asked, but I didn't reply.

All day we waited, while the sun moved the shadows through the empty grass. Some shadows walked and stopped by the fountain, gazing at us before walking on once more. He told me how the shadows thrown by the fires he stoked reminded him of the lives other boys must lead, lives he would never know anything about. Sleeping, never far from his father's calloused hands, he had longed for a friend, but could never picture what that friend might be like. A siren wailed in the distance and the city's hum rose like a final breath. What is happening? he asked, and curled his fingers round me. Nothing, I answered. Be calm.

Towards afternoon I must have slept. I imagined a moth fluttering towards the sun, the dust on its wings crackling with the heat, the flame spurring him on to his own extinction. When I awoke the mauve light had softened the shadows and given each colour a life of its own. It was evening.

The boy stood on the stone petal staring at the sky. I swung my way towards him, wrapped one arm around his torso and flew. I held his face close to mine to see the passing wonders echoed in his eyes. I bore him round at random and my desire became delight. The rush of wind drew my hair around him in a silken cloak. We flew together, out by the southern suburbs. We went far up into those realms of pure air where the rose-coloured clouds hung over the city I had loved like a brooding mushroom. The winds were fresh and keen up there. The air was aquamarine. I could see the lines of the bay very dimly, and another line too, between the metal green I knew to be the sea and the brownish mass that was the city. I sped down towards it and found not one line but two, both of which crossed at intervals, in slender figures of eight. It was the railway-track, which traced the curve of the bay. I had heard tell of these tracks, but had never yet seen them. His eyes were alert to every passing shape, as if the shadows his flaming coals threw had taken on true life. This side of the city was foreign to me, with its multitude of cramped, cracked villas tumbling towards the sea. I bore us closer to the land and found the houses gave way to a slope of trees. Though there was foliage at the tops, the trunks were quite bare and so I whipped between them, grazing the peeling

bark like a swallow. The dance of those trees I appre-
hended without thought as I threaded my way through
them and crept upwards again. We burst through the
foliage and the odour there – thicker than steel wool,
richer than pollen – brought to mind the one I had last
held this close. I thought of musk once more. The moun-
tainside sang of it and told me my desire had an object.
The slope became a cliff, wreathed in fog. The fog bled
downwards and I followed to the sea where our reflec-
tions rippled with our movement. Then there was fog
no more and tracks beneath us. We passed scattered
villas, imitative of a style I could not now remember.
They led to a bridge, and a station beyond.

I felt the panic of a desire that had led me truly. I traced
a large arc over the eaves of the station. There was a line
of pleasure-parlours by a crumbling promenade. In one
of them a yellow light glimmered.

28

She was standing by the dodgems in a blue smock. There were blotches on her face and runnels of hair along her arms. The changes, she told me, were so rapid that each day was a source of sometimes wonder, sometimes terror, sometimes both. She had longed to see me, but had been unwilling to approach, since she felt the need of a partner to delight in them. Could you now? she asked, and came towards me, the pits and shallows of her face raised in expectation. Yes, I said, but the word that emerged did not seem affirmative. So, she said, I must find another. She brushed my translucent face with her bunched fingers. Business was even worse, she told me, in the realms of entertainment than in the realm of perfume. Her friends had shunned her, she told me, seeing her as a sign, of a happening they would never allude to or define. And yet I am glad, she said. Tell me why I am glad. The fact, I told her, is a relief from its anticipation. And the feeling is all. She drew her swollen lips into a smile. Once more, she understood. A soldier entered then, his head bent low, his hands thrust deep into his khakis. You must leave now, she whispered. She drew her smock around her face and walked towards him.

We slipped through the shadows, the boy and I. I

drew him over the awning in one sad curve. The soldier parted her tresses below us. She sighed with anticipated pleasure. We hovered above them, like uninvited guests, until I drew him towards the sea once more.

29

The waters were calm, a long shallow pit of salt. All hint of reflection had now vanished. They were graced by a thin pall of mist.

You cannot blame her, the boy said. His voice bounced over the waters.

No, I replied. I sank with him to just above that mist.

She loved you, he said. But only for a time.

His wisdom was comforting. I fell with him into the sea and held him there, buoyed by an excess of salt.

He remarked on how it tasted like tears. I agreed with him. We let the sea carry us, and the night.

30

꼰꼰꼰꼰꼰

When day came up, we saw that the city with its crumbling cubes was far behind us. The waters steamed gently.
The liquid rose in a diaphanous haze and left behind
pure crystals of salt. They stayed poised beneath the
surface like a thousand eyes. I twined myself into a vessel
beneath him and moved us forwards with my broad
fingers. He told me of the mermaid who had ventured on
land and to whom each footstep was like the thrust of a
blade. Soon my arms became covered in a crystal sheen.

The sun moved slowly on the waters. At its pinnacle
the haze was such that it multiplied itself. I swam on.
The boy wondered whether the sun moved backwards
out here. But no, it was merely the illusion of haze.

I felt little need to speak. The sound of the water,
oddly reverberant in the ever-present vapour, made
speech enough. The boy talked as the spirit moved him.
He had strands of my hair wrapped around his fists, in
excitement or anticipation. Then night came down and
the light gave way quite unobtrusively.

31

❧❧❧❧❧❧

We must have slept, for I awoke to moonlight and a
sense of turbulence. The sea all about us was calm, however, and the moon was brilliant in the absence of haze.
The boy still slept. I heard a prodding all around me
which merged into a voice. I saw Alarth winging towards
me across the waters. Come, come, he whispered. A
winged fish broke the surface, twisted silver under the
moonlight and enveloped him in its maw. Then a white
flash filled the air from the city we had left. It was paler
than any white that had been and was followed by others,
each paler again till the white seemed permanent. Then
the sounds came, all the sounds at once, from the deepest to the thinnest in a circular boom, they sang towards
us in waves, and hard on their heels the waters followed.
I covered the boy and was dragged by the mountain of
water.

32

What came was not quite daylight and not quite night. The waters were calm and strewn with debris and cut grass. I had twined myself into a pouch round the boy. Far behind us that cloud, shaped like a phoenix, glowed with that terrible mauve. I stroked my fingers and moved us towards a promontory beyond.

A marble arm lay on the whitened sand. The boy was sick, I knew. His translucent lips tried to speak, but couldn't. I rose with him from the waters and made my way across that sand. There were the marks of feet. A fish twined its way round a clump of seagrass, its gills moving easily. I followed the webbed footprints.

When the time came that I knew the boy was dying, I wrapped myself fully round him, assumed him into myself. We both walked onwards, though my steps were weary with the knowledge that I would never see his face again. I remembered the cornheads, but felt no need for food. After a time those footprints were joined by others.

Each knew where to go, with no need of direction. With the mareotic sea far behind me, I took their advice. Many, many footprints later I came to a pool. The boy in me drew me to its surface. I put my lips to it and drank and felt his satisfaction. When the rippling caused by my lips had settled, I saw a reflection there, no less terrible than mine. A hand rubbed white sand away from a mouth. It was like mine in its shape and texture. Her hair, unmistakably female, was a whey-coloured fan in the constant wind. I raised my head and the boy inside me leapt. Her lips moved slowly and creased themselves upwards. My lips moved too. I recognised Marianne.

33

We spoke for a while, by the pool. Once accustomed to each other's voices, we both walked together, following the footprints before us. We had similar memories of the mareotic lake. She told me of a fish that walked and of a tree that shed its covering of scales. Matilde, she told me, was inside her now. I put my arms down to her waist and felt her. The boy kicked with pleasure at the touch.

Once a large beast flew above us and her hand gripped mine. We followed the footprints, but met no others. Soon the sands gave way to a vista of grass. The labour of our feet was lessened then, that soft cushion drew us onwards. The footprints had ceased, but we followed our own path. We crossed a hill and found a landscape of tall poplars. Planted years ago, it seemed to speak of quieter times. If things lead us to anything, she said to me, they surely lead us to realisation. Each happening bears a message, as surely as those poplars speak of whoever planted them. She curled her fingers round my hand once more and I saw the translucence was slowly fading, being replaced by something like a tan. The line of poplars led us to a signpost reading: HOPE ETERNAL. The arrow had wound itself into a circle, though, the point of which pressed into its rear. There was a garden up ahead. The gates were unattended and the grasses wild. The sundial seemed bleached by an eternity of light and the sprinklers moved so slowly that they whispered. Can I kiss you, she asked and I answered yes, in a voice that had become like hers. She had to tilt her head to reach my lips which I found were once more soft. The kiss was long, long enough for the sun to cross the dial, for the moon to traverse it and for the sun to rise once more. I saw the globes of her eyes and in my visage reflected there saw something as human as surprise.